"I guess you were right, Rebekkah. That sermon tonight was for both of us.

"You pray for me and I'll pray for you," André went on, "and we'll believe that God can bring a reconciliation about. How's that?"

Rebekkah nodded. "Better be careful what you pray for, André."

André smiled. "Oh, I am. Believe me, I am."

And he was certain he was going to be praying for God to help him find more time to spend around this woman....

Books by Cheryl Wolverton

Love Inspired

A Matter of Trust #11
A Father's Love #20
This Side of Paradise #38
The Best Christmas Ever #47
A Mother's Love #63
*For Love of Zach #76
*For Love of Hawk #87
*For Love of Mitch #105
*Healing Hearts #118
*A Husband To Hold #136
In Search of a Hero #166

*Hill Creek, Texas

CHERYL WOLVERTON

RITA Award finalist Cheryl Wolverton has well over a dozen books to her name. Her very popular HILL CREEK, TEXAS series has been a finalist in many contests. Cheryl grew up in Oklahoma, lived in Kentucky, Texas and now Louisiana, but she and her husband of twenty years and their two children, Jeremiah and Christina, consider themselves Oklahomans who have been transplanted to grow and flourish in the South. Readers are always welcome to contact her via: P.O. Box 207, Slaughter, LA 70777 or e-mail at Cheryl@cherylwolverton.com. You can also visit her Web site at www.cherylwolverton.com.

In Search of a Hero
Cheryl Wolverton

Love Inspired®

Published by Steeple Hill Books™

STEEPLE HILL BOOKS

Steeple
Hill™

ISBN 0-373-87173-2

IN SEARCH OF A HERO

Copyright © 2002 by Cheryl Wolverton

All rights reserved. Except for use in any review, the reproduction
or utilization of this work in whole or in part in any form by any
electronic, mechanical or other means, now known or hereafter
invented, including xerography, photocopying and recording, or in
any information storage or retrieval system, is forbidden without
the written permission of the editorial office, Steeple Hill Books,
300 East 42nd Street, New York, NY 10017 U.S.A.

All characters in this book have no existence outside the imagination of
the author and have no relation whatsoever to anyone bearing the same
name or names. They are not even distantly inspired by any individual
known or unknown to the author, and all incidents are pure invention.

This edition published by arrangement with Steeple Hill Books.

® and TM are trademarks of Steeple Hill Books, used under license.
Trademarks indicated with ® are registered in the United States Patent
and Trademark Office, the Canadian Trade Marks Office and in other
countries.

Visit us at www.steeplehill.com

Printed in U.S.A.

Jesus looked at them and said, "With man this is impossible, but with God all things are possible."
—*Matthew* 19:26

Mom—It's been 12 books and you're still reading them and even tickled with all of the overseas copies. Thank you for your support. I love you.

Anita, you had no idea how wonderful Titan could be. Now you'll have to watch for your new baby, Katie, in a book! I love you. To my other siblings, Deb and James, thanks for telling me you like my books!

To my family, Steve, Christina, Jeremiah and the unofficial family Darrell Stevens (who might as well be family the way he lives over here—grin) and in-laws Phyllis, Me Maw, John, John II, Michelle, Ross, Diana, Leigh and Randy.

Prologue

The information was out in the open again.

She had been told it wouldn't be found, that it was buried for good. With her help, they'd managed to cover everything up.

Why had she done it?

She should have let them take their chances, but at the time, it had seemed like the right thing to do. The right way to go.

Hanging up the phone, she turned, sighing and heading toward the stairs. "What am I going to do? This will ruin everything!"

She didn't see the shadow of a person she passed on her way upstairs.

Chapter One

The sweltering heat of the humid Texas night clung to André Watson as he lounged on the bench in Colundra Park in the downtown city of Hamilton. He waited for the meeting his contact had set up.

He wondered just how out of the ordinary he looked in the khaki pants and dark green polo shirt. Especially at this time of night.

Twisting his arm, he again checked his watch. Nearly ten.

Two years ago André had thought by this time he'd be married, settled down and on his way to having children with Sarah. Sarah whom his father had deceived, Sarah who had hit rock bottom and ended up at her brother-in-law's house, Sarah who had married Justin and had a seven-year-old niece-step-daughter and now, through modern miracles, had her own child on the way.

He'd lost Sarah, left the family business and started out on his own, a business dedicated to helping the poor, the needy, not the rich class like his father did. Two years ago seemed like a lifetime.

A lifetime in which he had catered to the rich, not the poor—which was why he sat here now at nearly ten on a Friday night. Had he not started his own business after his father had ruined his engagement to Sarah he would be at home now, watching TV, getting ready to go to bed for the night and maybe play a round of golf in the morning…

So many things had changed. Looking back, he wondered how he'd been so shallow and empty and not seen it.

He would never have been caught dead out this time of night to meet a contact. And not in this part of the town.

André glanced at the overhead light, one of many that dotted the cement path winding its way through the huge park. He again told himself he was doing the right thing. He'd let go of Sarah, wishing her well with the man who had stolen her heart. He'd even, to a point, admitted the only reason he'd dated Sarah was he'd been in love with the idea of settling down and having children. He'd been searching for something to fill his emptiness—he'd just been searching in the wrong area. Sarah hadn't been for him.

He'd even forgiven his stepbrother who, though he hadn't worked full-time in the business at that time, had sided with his father over the firing of Sarah.

What he couldn't forgive was his father's actions or get over the hurt his father had caused by refusing to admit that what he'd done was wrong.

A sluggish wind whispered through the bushes, moving the humid air around in the suburb that was well outside the Fort Worth Dallas area. It did nothing to cool him off as he shifted impatiently.

Tailor-made suits had given way to khakis and jeans as he'd moved into the slums to represent the less fortunate. It seemed like another lifetime—a lifetime his father enjoyed reminding him of as he insisted André get over his snit and come back to work for him.

But André refused, for many reasons, the least of which was his father wouldn't admit he had been wrong. So here he sat, waiting in the semidarkness, sweat trickling down his back, wishing the hundred-degree heat would finally break and bring some relief to the area.

He was waiting on a contact that had information on something that would really interest him, or so he'd been told. What it was he couldn't imagine, but many contacts in the past had come through for him, especially the one he was waiting on, so he wouldn't leave until the tardy man showed up. The slight sound of sneakers on cement caught his attention, drawing his gaze to his unhurried contact.

"Hey, man, you been waiting long?"

André heard the drawl of Billy Redford as he came idling up. Tall and slim, Billy wore pants that were way too big, held up with a belt cinched in around his middle, and a tank top that had seen better days. The cap on his head was turned, the bill pointed down and to the right—always the same direction, same color, same tilt to the hat. Billy dropped down on the bench next to André.

"What do you think, Billy? We were supposed to meet thirty minutes ago," he said impatiently. It was too hot to be impatient, he realized, and glanced across the park, willing himself to relax. Billy had good information. He usually did. Getting upset wouldn't hurry the man. More than likely it would slow him down.

Few people could be seen wandering the park. In the distance he heard the occasional horn or someone's loud laughter that broke through the night. Other than that, it was eerily quiet. Most couples, and singles for that matter, traveled into Fort Worth for the evening on a Friday night.

"I got caught up, man. You know you

didn't have to wait. A man with the color of your skin this time of night could just get himself into major trouble out here, ya know?''

''I live in this neighborhood now, Billy. I doubt because I'm Caucasian anyone is going to pick me off.'' Of course, that wasn't necessarily true, André thought, but he wouldn't admit that to Billy. He wanted to help in the lower income area. He ignored the voice that said he still had bitterness toward his father that had partially been responsible for landing him where he now practiced.

Billy never met André's eyes, his gaze constantly roving as he reached under his shirt and pulled out a manila folder, dropping it between them. That's how Billy was. He was never still, always moving, his gaze never settling on one thing. Tall, slender, black, he was at least five years André's senior.

And he was right. André needn't have waited, except he had nothing at home waiting for him, no one there to welcome him, nothing at all. "Yeah, well," André countered, "you said it was important. Your client was sure I'd want this."

André lifted the folder to look in it, but Billy stopped him. "Where's my payment?"

"I see the goods, you get paid," André replied mildly, thinking they went through this every time Billy brought him information. It was standard practice.

Billy released the envelope. "I think you'll find some interesting stuff in there."

"Reading the mail again?" André murmured as he opened the papers to peruse just what was in them.

"Nah. But I have ears."

"This life is gonna get you in trouble one day, Billy. You need to go legit," André said and then sat forward as he realized what the papers covered.

"My money?" Billy prompted.

"Who gave you this stuff?" André demanded, his gaze going to Billy, his heart starting to hammer loud in his ears.

"Hey, that ain't part of the deal, man," Billy protested. "I can't reveal my sources. I just deliver the goods and get paid."

"This is different." To André, at least, it was. This was about him, about his father, about the past.

"Not to me it ain't," Billy muttered. "I tell on my sources, I don't get the business."

André forced himself to calm down and pulled an envelope from his back pocket "Tell your contact I want to meet him."

"I'll do that," Billy said, snatching the envelope. Just as quickly it disappeared from his hand under his shirt. Billy hurried off, leaving André sitting there holding the information that might just prove that his almighty father wasn't perfect. That he could make mistakes. Of course, if it was true, it could also ruin *his* reputation, but all André could think about was the fact this might finally make his dad see things differently. It might finally make him admit he could be wrong.

But how?

André continued to sit there and stare at the information until an idea bloomed in the back of his mind, an idea that he didn't really cotton to at first as it crawled up and presented itself, but an idea just the same. It was an idea that, as he forced himself to look at it and examine it objectively, might really work.

If André could only get his dad to go along with him.

And if the information wasn't simply a pack of lies. Either way, this was something that couldn't be ignored, and whether André liked the idea or not, it was a way to find out if this information was the truth.

His dad would probably love his plan.

André wasn't sure how he felt about it.

But to see his family name like this, in these papers, and the consequences it would cause if it were true...

He had to do it.

Chapter Two

"Your father is busy. Is there something I can help you with?"

Rebekkah Hawkley stood poised by the elevators, ready to deter André Watson from going into his father's office, if at all possible. She hated it when André showed up. He always put Drydan in such a foul mood, and then she had to work with an angry man for the rest of the day.

"Hello, Rebekkah," André murmured with a smile, turning on the charm that usually got him past the secretaries in the building. Had Wanda not contacted Rebekkah,

André would probably have made it all the way past Shirley and Mary and be in there right now, once again arguing with his father about some silly case.

The smile he had could warm anyone to his way of thinking if they weren't careful. She'd seen him use it on jurors before. Tall, slender, golden hair like his mother, Margaret DuMoiré Watson, André had had it all, until he had a falling out with his father.

"Hello, André," she replied and waited to see what he would say next.

She'd heard the story of what happened with his father. Supposedly, Drydan had fired André's fiancée worried that André had taken time off to avoid seeing Sarah for some reason. Some sort of problem between the two had rocked the foundation of their relationship, according to office talk.

Drydan worried about his son and had thought he was helping him. But André had reacted in anger, leaving the practice, breaking Drydan and Margaret's heart. The only good thing that had come of it was that it left an opening for an up-and-coming lawyer—her—and had gotten Drydan's stepson, Michael, more involved in the business. He wasn't a lawyer, but he did assist in research and such for Drydan—he had for nearly seven years now, since he'd come to live with the Watsons. After the falling out between André and his father, Michael had gone to work full-time for his father.

"Tell me, Rebekkah, are you still gofering for my father?"

Rebekkah's eyes narrowed. André was great at distractions. He got to know his opponent and knew how to attack. That's what made him a good lawyer. Unfortunately, it had made him cynical in many ways, too, she believed. "You know I don't gofer for anyone, André. I'm a lawyer in my own right, and your father respects that."

André snorted. "Yeah. Just like he does me."

"You know he only wants you back in the business," Rebekkah argued. "That's why he's always on you to get out of the inner city." Sighing with exasperation she asked, "Why do you come here to cause

Drydan problems? Your constant attacks wear him down.''

André at least, had the grace to shift uncomfortably. In khaki pants and light blue shirt with the sleeves rolled halfway up, André even looked good when he was uneasy. That unsettled her, as well. He shouldn't look so good. However, she was glad she'd scored a point and ruffled that calm exterior. It gave her a feeling of control, something she rarely felt when André Watson was in the same room.

Or she thought she had scored a small triumph until he continued. ''You're naive, Rebekkah. You can't believe everything Pastor Jacob says about forgiveness. Sometimes things have to be taken into our own hands.''

Sadly, she shook her head. So much for thinking she had unsettled him. He still thought of her as the green kid at the firm, the one who didn't know what Drydan was really like. ''You're too bitter, André.'' Stubbornly she added, ''I think I'll have a talk with Jacob Sunday and mention he should take a small amount of time to preach forgiveness again.'' She paused significantly then added, ''*If* you agree to show up, that is.'' It concerned Drydan that André rarely went to church. At least Drydan seemed to have changed and cared more since he lost André to his own practice.

André shrugged. ''Talk to Jacob?'' he asked mildly. She knew he saw right through her lie. She had never been able to bluff André. She'd known him impersonally for nearly six months, and yet he still had the capacity to drive her crazy. He was a good man except for the blind spot he had about his father. ''I go sometimes,'' André said, absently waving off her comment.

He was a good man except for his blind spot about his father *and* church, she amended.

Abruptly André's tone changed. ''Believe it or not, Rebekkah, I'm not here to argue with my father but to work on a case we have to reopen.''

Rebekkah gaped at André trying to determine if she'd heard the man right. Finally, when she recovered her voice, she asked, "You're going to work for your father?"

"Isn't that what I just said?" he murmured, that smirking little smile appearing as his head tilted down toward her slightly and his eyebrows transformed into that certain angle as he gave her a superior look.

Using the time to smooth her peach jacket and straight skirt, Rebekkah regrouped. "I don't believe it."

"Why don't you come with me to Dad's office and you'll find out if I'm telling the truth." He baited her knowing how she had planned to turn him down the hall in another direction, to another office, anywhere but Drydan's. However, what would he do if she called his bluff?

"You don't think I will, do you?" She hated the way this cool, calm golden boy always rattled her.

Slipping his hands in his pockets, he said, "I'm hoping you will."

She studied him, trying to discern the truth behind the neutral gaze he leveled at her. Was he serious? Did he really plan to come to work for his father again? Or was this simply a trick to see his dad? She couldn't remember a time both hadn't ended up in an argument.

Why couldn't André accept that his dad had changed since the day his son had left? Though Rebekkah hadn't known him well then, she did know that losing André as he had caused a wound within him. A wound that couldn't heal because they couldn't talk out the problem. She knew André still wasn't over Sarah. She'd heard through the grapevine how he avoided places she frequented. He told everyone he was over it, but his hate toward his father supported a different story. Which brought her back to André's motivations. Was he really interested in just talking this time?

There was no telling how long they would have stood in a face-off if they hadn't been interrupted.

"Well, well, if it's not the prodigal brother returned, not to rejoice, however, but to slink into the fold like a wolf hunting more prey."

Rebekkah winced at Michael's words.

"Well, hello to you, too, brother," André drawled.

There was certainly no love lost between the two brothers, Rebekkah thought, exasperated with how this meeting had changed into a confrontation of kin. At least this fight wasn't on André's side, Rebekkah reminded herself wearily. Michael didn't care at all for Drydan's son, who seemed to always get preferential choice over the stepson. André acted as if he had no idea that it bothered Michael at all.

"How are you doing, Michael?" André smiled benignly at the other golden boy in the office, as Rebekkah thought of him. Michael looked much like André in color and build. The only real differences were the square jaw and the dark brown eyes instead of the deep piercing silver gray ones that André had. There was no doubt both were Margaret's children. The smoother lines of André's facial structure, aristocratic nose and silver gray eyes came from Drydan.

"Actually, I was doing great until I heard

you had come here to harass your father again.''

Rebekkah noted how some of the employees down the hall seemed to be migrating toward them—obviously to see a family feud in progress. Rebekkah decided to put a stop to it right here and now. Part of her job was to keep Drydan happy. Knowing his employees were getting an eyeful in his firm wasn't going to bring that about. ''He's here to help his father, he says, Michael. Why don't we go talk with Drydan?'' she offered, turning to André and drawing his attention to her.

''I thought you'd never ask,'' André replied and gave her a sweet smile.

Michael showed his disgust with the curling of his lip.

''Michael,'' she said, ''I need that report on the Keller Water Treatment Facility and how that case turned out—in detail. I'm going to trial in a few weeks and have decided to use the Muller versus the City of Keller case as precedent. Can you do a workup for me?''

Michael hesitated then nodded curtly. "Sure thing, Rebekkah." Leveling one last disgusted look at his stepbrother, Michael turned and left.

"Looks like he's as happy as ever," André murmured as he started down the long carpeted hall toward his father's office.

"He's just gotten used to working full-time here, André. He's settled in," Rebekkah said quietly. They passed the tall mirrors and portraits of others who had once worked in the office, as well as doors that led to secretaries and legal assistants. Though they were a small firm by many standards, they were the largest firm outside the Fort Worth firms. Cherry-wood tables with floral arrangements dotted the hall as they approached Drydan's office. "I imagine Michael worries that you'll come waltzing back into the firm, and he'll no longer be the number one son."

André sighed. "I don't think of Michael like that. True, I didn't know him most of my life until his father died and he moved in with us, but I've always accepted him."

Rebekkah strolled along beside André, her worry over André's desire to confront his father shifting to André's situation with his brother. "I know you have. I think it's something Michael will have to work through. Be patient." With a nod they passed the private secretary's desk.

"Trying to comfort me?" André asked mildly, pausing outside Drydan's office door.

Rebekkah bristled. Turning to meet his gaze, she replied, "No way. You have too many women around here that would love to do that. I'm simply pointing out the Christian thing to do."

André chuckled. "The Christian thing. Something you aren't going to let me forget, are you, Rebekkah, love?"

She reached for the handle of one of the double doors then smiled sweetly—too sweetly. "Not a chance. It gives me great pleasure to remind you daily about forgiveness." Turning, she pushed the door open, a smile on her dark face. "Drydan, your son is here to see you."

Chapter Three

"André what brings you here?" Drydan studied his son carefully, the wariness showing plainly on his face.

André noted Rebekkah come into the office with him, closing the door after she was in. He knew his father didn't need moral support, but he had to hand it to Rebekkah. She was loyal.

"Hello, Father. We need to talk."

"If you've come to argue, son—" Drydan began.

"Not at all," André said, and crossed the carpeted floor to drop into a plush maroon

brocaded chair in front of his father's desk.
André had grown up in these offices. From
the time his father had been an associate until he'd bought out the major shares and run
the entire law firm, André had played in
these halls. His only desire had been to one
day be at his father's side, cleaning up the
world for good people to live. As he'd
grown up here, he'd learned all about the
business. They had lawyers that specialized
in all kinds of things. André had decided
early on he wanted to work with civil law.
And he had seen that dream come true. He
had enjoyed it...most of the time. Except
when his father started to insist things be
done a certain way, that they could only take
high-profile cases and on and on. In actual-
ity, leaving had given him freedom he hadn't
had at Watson and Watson.

"André said he had a proposal to discuss
with you," Rebekkah prompted as she
moved beside André and seated herself in
the other chair.

She really was a pretty young woman, her
black hair hanging straight and curling

slightly under on the ends. She was tall, willowy and slender, and her dark brown eyes and smooth complexion reminded him of a pampered socialite instead of a lawyer. Rebekkah was very careful of her appearance. Reluctantly, he returned his attention to his father. Though he was here and planned to bring up something that he hoped would eventually force his father's hand, he couldn't help the feelings deep within that reminded him this was his father, the man who had raised him.

His life hadn't been bad like it had for some of his clients, who often told him their stories. His father simply insisted on complete control. This was unacceptable in many ways. A small part of him, the part that had grown up loving his father, warned him that if he hurt his father in retaliation for all his father had done, he would hurt himself, as well.

But he had to do it. It had to be done. His dad had to admit this time he'd gone too far. If he could do that without that eternal hurt then fine, otherwise… Pushing that from his

mind André shifted and said, "I do, Dad.
Remember the Kittering Lumber suit several
years back that this firm handled?"

"The Alaska case," Drydan said. Sitting
back in the tall leather chair, he crossed his
gray-clad legs. The charcoal gray suit was
tailored to his tall figure, and he looked
daunting in it, the way he sat just so as if
in deep thought. It was a pose André knew
well, one his father had grown accustomed
to taking when discussing a case. "A group
of townspeople was trying to prove the lumber plant was causing cases of cancer."

"A lumber plant causing cancer?" Rebekkah asked, curiosity rife in her voice.

André allowed his gaze to touch Rebekkah's. "They treat the wood there. Chemicals were involved. I handled a lot of the
work on that case." André forced his gaze
away from Rebekkah and back to his father.
André noted he enjoyed looking at her. In
church, whenever he went, he'd thought it
was simply because she sat nearly directly
across from him. However, here she wasn't
sitting across from him. Here she was sitting

next to him, showing interest in a case he'd once worked on. Most women wouldn't care what the case was about, but she did. He saw it in her gaze as it went from his father to him and back. He found that interest challenged him to explain more. However, his father jumped in.

"So what does that have to do with us now?" Drydan asked impatiently. "We proved the group was wrong and our clients had not poisoned the lake in that area. Things ended great, and we still have them as our clients today, bringing in quite a bit of money for us, because of that win."

André turned to his father. "Word has reached me that someone doctored information. And it seems that there are people out there getting ready to reopen the case."

Drydan harrumphed. "Nonsense."

"My sources are fairly certain of this. They warned me that this company and all involved in it are a possible target for suit in a cover-up."

Drydan paused. The gray-haired man wearing the custom-tailored suit, the man who usually chewed up the competition and spit them out, paused and studied his son. "It's a ridiculous charge," he argued, but there was hesitation in his voice.

"You know that and I know that, Dad, but you're the one who taught me that reputation is important. A high-profile case like this reopening could cause irreparable damage to the company."

"So why come to me about this? I would think you'd love to see this company go under."

André stiffened. Here it came. He and his dad couldn't sit down without it turning into an argument. His dad wouldn't accept him since he'd left the business. He had to poke at André to provoke him until they ended up arguing. "You know that's not true, Dad. I only want you to admit you were wrong about firing Sarah."

"She lied to you."

André's lips tightened as the old feelings surfaced, as bitterness rose. "She didn't lie, she simply hadn't told me the truth—at first."

"Same thing," Drydan said with a wave of his hand.

André's temper heated even more at that simple dismissal of his feelings.

"I think we should stick to the problem here," Rebekkah broke in.

Drydan nodded, and André knew now why Rebekkah was there. She was there to run interference over anything his father might not want to get into. Give her a point for initiative. "Right you are, Rebekkah," Drydan replied.

Though André would like to finish this and somehow force his father to admit he was wrong, he reminded himself to stick with what he was doing. If he could get his dad to admit he was wrong about this case, then maybe... "I worked on that case, Dad. It's my reputation as much as yours on the line here. I thought perhaps we could work together on this, go back over the information that was presented and check out everything on our end before the case is reopened so we can nip this in the bud."

"They won't find anything," Drydan

said, then paused. "But that might be a good idea. Just, um, what did your contact give you to bring you running over here?"

That was his dad, always the lawyer. "An interoffice memo from Kittering Lumber insisting that nothing be said on the subject, and it just so happens to mention Marcus Langley in it as putting out those orders."

"He is the owner. There's nothing unusual about that."

"True, but couple that with the fact that there is a newspaper article saying Marcus knew nothing about what was going on up there. If I remember correctly, he swore that under oath. But this memo was written before the trial. I'm not sure, and it's flimsy, but someone has decided to go back and revisit the site. My contact also said there is new evidence that has turned up that will prove Kittering's parent Company, Langley International, did indeed assist in a cover-up."

"Like what?" His father's eyes cut sharply to him, intense with his need to know every detail.

"I don't have that information. The contact only said to go back over the old records and to search deeply before our career ended up ruined."

Actually, it had said before André's career was ruined, but his father didn't know it had been so personal. "What I want to do, Dad, is go back over the old cases, prepare a review on them. I'd like to see what we can find from then until now."

"Does this mean you'll be coming back?" his dad asked.

André hesitated. "I'm not giving up my own practice. You could have someone here work with me as a liaison. Someone who can be a go-between."

"I'd rather you come back here, son."

"I need to be out on my own," André argued quietly.

His father's lips tightened in anger. Then he nodded curtly. "Rebekkah can work with you on this. I'm adding you back on the payroll while you do this, though."

"Dad…"

"That's nonnegotiable. If you're going to

help clear up whatever this is then you're on the payroll.''

Well, that compromise was better than André had hoped for the outcome of this meeting. He had thought his dad might refuse outright unless he came back to work for them. "Thanks, Dad."

Drydan stood. "Thanks for bringing this to our attention," he said.

André stood, as well, and headed for the door. "Guess this just might prove you aren't always right, Dad," he said.

Drydan flushed.

André continued before his father could comment. "I'll find all the information I can and get started tomorrow."

Rebekkah, who had been relatively quiet until now, called, "You will need to check with me about my schedule. I'm in court tomorrow. Perhaps the next day."

André paused and turned. His eyebrow went up. Surprised, he worked to curb a smile. Though it had been a while since he dated, he knew a rebuke from a woman when he heard one. He should apologize for his presumptuous attitude. She was probably miffed about the shot he'd taken at his father. But instead he baited her. "I can work on it tomorrow while you're in court."

"Nonsense," Drydan said. "If she's the liaison I want her there with you working."

Patience, André admonished himself. "Until then," he said and started toward the door.

"I'll let you know what time," Rebekkah called.

Again, André paused, almost at the door. Turning, he met her smug gaze and smiled slowly. "Over dinner, because I'll be busy all day Tuesday."

When her smile collapsed and burgeoning surprise showed, he decided he'd scored his point. With a wave, he walked out the door and headed down the hall.

Rebekkah was forceful by nature, but she was going to learn when it came to being a lawyer she was way out of her league with him. He had a job to do and he'd do it.

Chapter Four

Brighton's was the perfect restaurant for a meeting. Quiet, dark, a place where they could talk and it wouldn't get out of hand.

Rebekkah liked that.

A lot.

It had taken five calls, four messages and two secretarial meetings before the two worked out their schedules. She could be as stubborn as he could about who would be in charge of this meeting.

Rebekkah felt she'd won. She swung her stocking-clad legs out of her car. Once standing, she shut the door behind her, wondering if André had arrived yet.

He'd wanted to meet at a local café. She'd nixed that idea, wanting to meet at the office over Chinese food—to which he'd said no.

Tan heels clicked across the dark asphalt as she headed toward the front door.

Of course, she'd known he wouldn't agree to the office. But at a place like this, she was certain he wouldn't pull any surprises—just what she'd hoped for.

Preparing for their first conversation since the one in Drydan's office, she had donned her tan linen suit that had darker brown threads woven through it, had pulled back her hair and brought her notebook with briefs on the case. She wanted André to know she was there strictly for business.

Why she let him bother her, she wasn't sure. But every time they were around each other her hackles went up.

As she approached the front of the building, she found her nemesis waiting.

He was dressed to kill, she thought despairingly. Wearing dark brown trousers with a lighter sports jacket, he looked all male.

Rebekkah winced as she realized what the problem was. She was attracted to this man.

She thought him too handsome for his own good.

Great. Physical attraction, she thought, disgusted. At least that was as far as it went. Of course, she didn't know him well enough for anything else, her mind reminded her—yet.

And that was the way it would stay.

"Good evening, Rebekkah. Shall we?" He motioned toward the door.

This was one thing she could do—court cases. Pulling her mind to that, she nodded. "I'm ready."

As she passed him, he murmured, "I'm sure you are."

Turning as they entered, she asked, "What do you mean by that?"

Eyebrows inching up, he said, "You're the type to do your homework."

Forcing herself to relax, she nodded.

The maître d' seated them, and the waitress took their orders. All was quiet before she spoke again.

"I trust you've had a good week?"

André smiled. "Never better. I really am beginning to enjoy my business in the inner city."

"Most people spend their life trying to escape there," Rebekkah said coolly. "I find it hard to believe you're enjoying work that pays next to nothing and small-time cases."

André tilted his head. "Is that how you see it, Rebekkah? That the little people aren't worth the work? I'm surprised."

Rebekkah had the grace to blush. "I—" She cleared her throat and continued, "I apologize, André. We once again have gotten off on the wrong foot. Actually, I've seen few lawyers who like working in the inner city. Most prefer a challenge that a bigger company represents—as well as the job security. I simply meant it's hard to believe after working with your father you'd find pleasure living from hand to mouth like that."

André continued to smile, his hands steepled in front of him as he studied her. "Do you peg all people like this before you get to know them or just me?"

Realizing she had no control over this conversation and wasn't going to gain control, she shook her head. "Again, I apologize."

André shook his head slightly. The candlelight brought out the golden tones in his hair and caused his eyes to twinkle with what looked like merriment. "Relax, Rebekkah. You came in here tonight prepared to do battle. I'm not sure why, but let's call a truce while we're together. Okay?"

Rebekkah hesitated. "I suppose I'm worried you're going to hurt your father again."

André's smile became strained. "I promise you, Rebekkah, I have no intention of hurting my father. I simply want him to admit he was wrong in breaking up my engagement. But, since we have to work together, I suggest we avoid that subject as much as possible. After all, if I'd wanted to hurt my father, I could have found a much easier way than coming to him with what I'd learned."

Rebekkah sighed and admitted he was right. Waving a hand, she nodded. "I've heard a lot about you, actually,'' she confessed.

''My father, I presume, has already flayed me alive?''

Rebekkah shook her head. ''Actually, no, André. He's proud of what you've accomplished. But since we are avoiding that subject,'' she said softly, ''what I meant was in court. I've heard you're competent and usually get what you set out to do.''

André nodded. ''I prefer civil cases, though I did assist my father in other areas as needed. I've backed off a lot of what I did when I first passed the bars.''

''What you were doing when you were involved in the Kittering case?'' Rebekkah asked.

André nodded. ''I used to be a trial lawyer,'' he admitted.

''I've researched the case and come up with a brief outline.''

''It was a simple enough case,'' André said, nodding his thanks as the waitress brought their tea and salads. He showed no discomfiture that she had researched a case he'd worked on or that she wanted to get right down to business. "A big company accused of not sticking to the EPA standards and poisoning the land around them. We proved the company was indeed within the bounds of the law."

"You proved that the poor people who had hired their lawyer didn't get a very good lawyer," Rebekkah countered. "Devil's advocate here," she added at his sudden scrutiny.

"Ah...well, perhaps." He played along.

"Enough that it might actually help them win the case if it's reopened in an appeal?"

André frowned. "Kittering had allegedly caused problems in the Alaskan wilderness with the fishing and water. There was proof that the number of fish the area produced was down. But then, the population was up and many more tourists had visited the area in the previous two years. There were minute amounts of their chemicals in the water, but nothing near what the EPA insisted Kittering keep their levels below."

"But what about the wildlife?"

Rebekkah said a quick prayer before picking up her fork and taking a bite of salad. André followed suit.

He had elegant hands, not the hands of a worker, but long gentle hands, she noticed. She thought of this Sunday when he'd shown up at church, when his friends had handed him their baby for a moment and how careful he had been. André was different from others she had met. And she knew many other male lawyers. Most were concerned about their careers and climbing the corporate ladder. Many played fast and loose. Rebekkah had clawed her way up that ladder, reveling when Drydan had taken her into the firm, even though she suspected it was to fulfill a minority quota.

She had a chance, at least.

And she wasn't going to blow it. Yet here sat André, a man raised in elegance, shrugging over his career, calm over the fact this case, if reopened, might damage his reputation and that of his family.

How he could be so at ease, she had no idea.

"If I remember correctly," André finally said, "there was never any direct proof that the deaths of those animals could be attributed to the drinking of the water—which was what the original lawsuit was about— the water contamination that was causing illnesses to so many in the area."

"Yes, but what if they've found a connection?" she asked. "I've gone through all the information I could find on the case. Your client was adamant that they had no idea of the pending lawsuit, thus could not have covered it up."

"On the day the Langley representative testified, it clearly indicates he didn't visit the site until after the lawsuit. And then he went up with the intention of finding out the truth," André said.

Rebekkah took another bite of her salad, frowning. "Is it possible someone forged the interoffice memo to make it look like the company was guilty when they weren't?"

André set his salad plate and fork aside. "I suppose so. We won't know until we see it. However, if someone did do that, then they'd surely know it would easily be proven a fake.''

When the waitress appeared with their seafood they both fell silent.

Once she was gone, André continued. ''I think it best we go on the assumption this is true and that someone is indeed going to visit the site for some new proof that we don't know about. I'd like to get to the bottom of this, too, find out if these people lied to us before we represented them.''

''If they did, and it comes out, whether you knew or not, it's still going to hurt your father terribly.''

André nodded. ''It will do that.''

''However, the poor people who've lost so many loved ones and fallen ill will have their proof.''

Again, he nodded. ''Which would be a good thing for some of them. I saw many at the time who were simply money-grubbing people who saw a chance to get rich. That was one reason I got out of being a trial lawyer. I got burned out really quick seeing the baser nature of people and their greed.''

"Not all poor people are money grabbers," Rebekkah said softly, her fork pausing by her plate.

"I agree. But we've represented many who were. Surely, Rebekkah, you've seen that in your experiences with my father's company."

Rebekkah's glance left André speechless.

André wouldn't let her escape, though. Reaching out, he caught her hand, which lay still on the table.

The warmth jolted her gaze to his. She froze, staring.

He didn't say anything, just continued to hold her hand.

"Yes, I've seen that in your father's business and in other businesses, as well," she finally admitted. "But I've seen the poor ones, as well, those who couldn't afford a lawyer and desperately needed help, the ones who weren't greedy and sought out help only to be turned down because they had no money."

"Which makes me wonder why you aren't more supportive of where I work," he murmured softly.

Realizing what she'd said, she pulled her hand back on the pretense of blotting her lips with the napkin. "If a person works, they can go places and not stay in the world they were born in. Many in the inner city just want to stay there."

André went back to eating. "Which means you really want to see me help them on their way, I suppose."

Rebekkah laughed. "You're good at twisting things around, André."

"And for a trial lawyer, Rebekkah, you can certainly jump from subject to subject."

The tension relieved, she smiled. "Simply to keep you confused."

"Oh, you do that without any problem," André said.

And she did, André thought, watching the way the woman blinked before smoothing all emotions from her soft complexion.

"So tell me, Rebekkah, what made you want a job like the one at Watson and Watson," André asked, deciding they'd discussed enough business for the night. He wanted to get to know his new partner better since they would be working together.

"I don't understand," she replied carefully. He thought most of her answers were careful, except to him. He'd noticed almost immediately he had the ability to rattle her easily. And he took advantage of it, too. "I mean, fast-paced, high stress, long hours."

"Oh." She smiled. The smile changed her features from beautiful to breathtaking. She really was quite a remarkable young woman. He had no idea how she'd stayed single so long, unless it was her sheer doggedness to climb the corporate ladder—something André realized wasn't worth it when he'd lost Sarah.

"I like the challenge. I love my job. It gives me a chance to challenge my mind and the laws. It also has the possibility of advancement, bigger cases and such."

"You want to make a name for yourself," he confirmed.

"I want to make sure I have a firm foundation to stand on and job security."

"Trusting God helps," he said.

She frowned. "Figures you'd quote things like that to me."

"I can't let you do all the quoting, now, can I?" he asked, enjoying the sparring.

"I saw you were in church Sunday," she countered.

"I was there, yes. But you didn't answer my question. Do you trust God to take care of you?"

"I believe a person has to put forth an effort, but yes, God will take care of me."

"Then it really boils down to you're running from or to something."

He'd struck gold with that, if the flash in her eyes was any indication. He wouldn't push it, though. At least now he had an idea why she seemed so determined to please his father and make a name for herself. "I've run, too, Rebekkah," he said simply. "I still am in some ways, I imagine. But that's what life is about, trials."

Tilting her head, she studied him. "Why do you really miss church, André?"

Steepling his hands in front of him, he smiled. "I'm backsliding, or so you say, Rebekkah."

"I'm wondering if there isn't more here than meets the eye."

He grinned. "Maybe you should find out."

Her cheeks reddened slightly, amusing him. Time to let her off the hook. He found teasing Rebekkah Hawkley too enjoyable. He didn't want to make her uncomfortable. "Can you get the transcripts together so we can go over them some evening?"

Clearly relieved to be on the subject of work, she pulled out her notebook and flipped through it. "That's going to be a tall order, but, yes, if you'd like."

"I'd like it very much. Let's meet somewhere quieter next time, more private, where we can spread out. Ideas?"

Rebekkah's brow furrowed, and she nibbled her lip before tentatively offering, "My place?"

He knew she expected him to say no and then they'd haggle like they had over this restaurant. Instead, he nodded. "Sounds fine."

He hid his smile as she gaped at him. "How about tomorrow night after church?"

"You'll be at church?"

"If you agree to the meeting afterward," he replied, smiling. He normally went to a much smaller church on Wednesday night, but he found he enjoyed talking with this woman. There was so much he didn't know about her. He'd barely scratched the surface and he found himself compelled to dig deeper, get to know her more. Missing one Wednesday night wouldn't hurt. His friend could take over the class for that night.

"What if I'm busy?" she challenged.

"But you won't be, will you, Rebekkah? Because you want me to be in church."

She chuckled. "It's not my job to see you show up."

"Nope. But it just might go a long way to helping me heal with my father, hey?"

She groaned.

He chuckled. "If you can't meet Wednesday, Rebekkah, then any day is fine. I'll still show up Wednesday night. How's that?"

"Why?" she asked, true puzzlement on her face.

"Because, Rebekkah Hawkley, you intrigue me, and though I have an engagement on Wednesdays I'll cancel it just to spend time with you.''

He'd done it again. The woman was gaping. Quickly recovering herself, she replied, ''Wednesday is fine for a meeting. I go in late on Thursdays, running errands, so actually that would be the best day.''

He nodded. ''Great.'' To himself he added, Go ahead and think by agreeing to the Wednesday meeting that you can pretend I didn't just say I was interested in getting to know you better. However, I'm not going to let you forget.

Crossing swords with Rebekkah was turning out to be quite fun. He found he was looking forward to peeling back another layer of the prickly woman and getting to know the female beneath.

For the first time since leaving his father's firm, he found his interests lay in the direction of pleasure and amusement instead of revenge.

What an odd, odd world, indeed.

Chapter Five

André was on the case.

With Rebekkah Hawkley.

He'd seen the sparks between the two.

There was more there than simply a case.

This could be used to his advantage.

It would definitely keep André close to the firm.

He would be able to watch the two, know what was going on, hear what was said.

And if they got too close, he'd also be able to make sure the truth didn't get out.

It was up to him.

And no matter what, he'd see the secret was safe.

* * *

"How can I help you?" Rebekkah asked, seating herself in front of Drydan's desk.

Drydan sat, surrounded by paperwork, gruff and busy. He finished writing something on a notepad and then pushed it aside.

Glancing up, he leaned back in his chair and rested an elbow on the armrest. "How'd the meeting with my son go last night?"

Rebekkah tucked her feet under the edge of the seat and smiled. "We discussed the case and agreed to get together after church tonight to go through the records."

Drydan scowled. "He's actually going to church?"

Rebekkah's smile stayed fixed, though she didn't feel like keeping it there. "I am getting the feeling there's a lot more to your son than meets the eye."

Drydan nodded and seemed to deflate right in front of Rebekkah. "Oh, there is. Believe me. I think the boy has finally decided on a path, and it doesn't include me."

Rebekkah took a deep breath. "Perhaps if you give it time..."

Drydan shook his head. "I have. And where has it gotten me? He's opened up his own practice, works daily to prove how wrong my firm is and specifically how wrong I am."

Touchy area, Rebekkah thought uneasily. Still, she had become close to Drydan since he'd hired her. Out of all the people she'd ever met, Drydan was more like a father figure to her than anyone else. Though she knew it was touchy, she just had to broach it. "He's still hurting over losing Sarah."

"Bushaw." Drydan used his favorite word when he disagreed with others. "He was in love with the idea of marrying and settling down. It's obvious. When it came out that Sarah was infertile, if he'd really loved her he wouldn't have taken off like he did. I simply did him a favor by firing the girl."

"You know that's not true, Drydan," Rebekkah reprimanded lightly.

Defensive, Drydan glared at her. "I was certain she was only out to get his money. At the time I felt it was the right thing to do."

"Have you ever considered you were wrong?" Rebekkah asked softly.

Drydan shoved his chair back. He shot to his feet and stalked across the room to open a small icebox. Rebekkah waited as he pulled out a bottle of water. Distractedly he twisted off the cap and snagged a glass, which he filled. After tossing a slice of lemon on top of his drink, he only took time to slam the door of the fridge before turning.

"I don't know." He finally answered Rebekkah's question. "You know things have changed since André left. I've had time to reconsider my actions, to see many of the areas I've messed up in, but André could have trusted that I wasn't purposely out to destroy his life."

"Perhaps he is old enough to make his own decisions, Drydan."

Drydan took a swig of his drink then shrugged. "I know that, but..."

"But you can't let go?"

He scowled. "I don't have much choice, do I?"

Rebekkah decided to try a different tack.

"Why don't you tell him that you've changed? Tell him about what happened in church and that you're consciously working to improve your business practices. Tell him that you made a mistake and if he's amenable, you're willing to try to start over."

"Religion is personal," Drydan argued. "If he can't see the change in me, then why tell him?"

"Because he's not working here and not around you enough to see what has taken place in your life," Rebekkah countered. She stood and moved across the room to where Drydan stood. Resting a hand on his arm, she said, "I know you hired me simply to fill a quota, Drydan. But you've given me a chance. You've helped me and taught me things that I couldn't have learned anywhere else. And during that time I like to think we've become…well, friends of a sort."

"You know I think of you more like a daughter than an employee," he muttered gruffly and then, unable to stand the show of emotion, he crossed the room and started rifling through papers again.

"Well, yes. And I feel the same way. That's why I have to tell you, Drydan, that you gave me a chance, and I think this thing between your son and you has the ability to heal. But both sides are going to have to give."

"I'm willing to give," Drydan retorted.

"I know you are," Rebekkah soothed. "But maybe not in the areas where he needs you to give."

"He wants me to tell him I was wrong." Drydan's flat tone told Rebekkah he knew that was the gist of the problem.

"And why is that a problem?"

"Because I wasn't."

Rebekkah thought about throwing up her hands in exasperation. Instead, before she could say a word, Drydan continued. "Look at the results of what has happened. He's alive again, not hidden behind a desk insisting that the world outside of this office doesn't exist."

"You want him back," Rebekkah reminded him.

"This is where he belongs," Drydan argued. "His mother and I were both worried, though. He had gotten to the point all he did was work and see Sarah. He had nothing else in his life. The first vacation he took was when Sarah rocked his world by telling him she couldn't have children."

"That would be hard for anyone to hear."

"You're telling me," Drydan said dryly. "I wanted grandchildren. Maybe I pushed the boy too hard in the responsibility part. That may be why he wanted to settle down with Sarah so desperately."

"Have you apologized to Sarah yet?"

Drydan shifted uncomfortably.

"You know, that might go a long way to healing your son's heart—to see you held no ill will against the woman you made a mistake about."

"She wasn't right for him. Her marrying Justin proves it. Look how happy she is now."

Rebekkah felt like she was banging her head against a brick wall. "Yes. She is. But your son isn't."

"Which brings me to the request I have."

Rebekkah realized only then that Drydan must not have come to the reason he'd called her to his office. She had thought he wanted to know about the meeting last night. She should have known better. Drydan probably had heard all about her meeting with his son from everyone in town by now. "What is that?" she asked him and moved over to take her seat, to brace herself.

Drydan finally faced Rebekkah, meeting her gaze head-on. What she saw in his eyes was a look of anguish and fear. It pained her to see this man hurting like this. How could one father and son become so separated?

She thought of her mother and had her answer—but then, that was different. Drydan had a job and loved his son; her mother...

"I want you to help me get my son back."

Rebekkah wasn't sure she heard him correctly until he continued.

"You're working on this case with him. You're going to be in contact with him almost daily. I want you to help him learn how to forgive me."

"I can't make him forgive you, Drydan."

Drydan waved an impatient hand. "I don't want that. I thought, well, by bridging the gap between us you could find a way to persuade him to come over some night to our house for dinner—with you, of course—on the pretext of discussing the case. Maybe through this he will see I'm not out to destroy him and we can at least open a line of communication."

Rebekkah shifted uneasily. "You want me to spy on him?"

"Not at all!" Drydan stiffened with offense. "He's my son. I wouldn't approve anyone spying on him. What I'd like is for you to befriend him. Maybe if he sees how you're treated here and how things have changed...and if we have a chance to have dinner together or something like that..."

Rebekkah saw desperation in Drydan's eyes. With that touch of humanity, she realized she couldn't deny him. Whether André realized it or not, Drydan loved him and wanted him back. She'd have to find a way to get both stubborn men to admit that there was fault on both sides. Then maybe they could start on the road to healing.

"Very well. I'll see what I can do."

Drydan stood from his desk and hurried around it. Pulling Rebekkah up, he gave her a hug. "Good girl. I don't know..." Releasing her, he cleared his throat. "You have no idea how much you've meant to me these past two years."

Rebekkah's heart constricted with emotion. "You've helped me, too, Drydan."

Drydan offered her a smile and then waved her off. "You'd better get back to work."

"Thank you," Rebekkah said. Grabbing her pen and the papers she'd brought into the office, she headed out the door.

"Don't forget. Dinner," he called after her.

"I won't."

"Drydan at it again?"

Rebekkah turned from closing the door to find Michael lounging in one of the chairs in the secretary's office. She passed Michael as she said, "At what, Michael?"

Michael stood and followed Rebekkah. "Schmoozing you. I think he's after information since you're working with my brother on this new case."

Rebekkah smiled as she strode down the hall. "Drydan is always after information. He likes to keep well informed on everything that goes on in his office. So what else is new?"

"He wants his golden boy back in the office so the firm can once again be Watson and Watson in practice," Michael said. His voice echoed with bitterness, causing Rebekkah to pause.

"Drydan is very glad you're here, Michael."

"I'm not a lawyer."

"No. But you're working your way up in the firm. He's offered to pay your way through college if you'd like."

"I know." Michael shrugged. "I don't know what I want," he finally confessed. "I do know, though, if André comes back I'll be out on the street again, just like when my mom married Drydan, leaving me with my deadbeat dad."

"Your dad wasn't a deadbeat at the time. I've heard you say so."

"Yeah. Whatever. So, what's next on the agenda for today? Have any interesting cases for me to research?" he asked, abruptly changing the subject.

"Not really. I would appreciate it if you'd gather all the information on the Kittering case you can find and put it in my car. I want to take it home and study it. André and I plan to go over it tonight after church."

"What's this about the Kittering case?" Michael asked sharply.

Rebekkah glanced at him in surprise. "That's the reason André and I are working together. It seems something has come up on the case. A possible cover-up from some part of the Kittering Corporation. Your father has assigned me as a liaison with André to work out the problem before the case is reopened."

Michael sneered. "Just like good old Dad. A way to get his errant son back. And if he finds it, he will of course be the hero to Watson and Watson once again and Drydan will do whatever necessary to make sure André knows it."

At her office Rebekkah paused. "You know, Michael, that attitude doesn't help your case with Drydan. He cares for you and has made room for you in the business. The least you could do is understand that his love isn't limited only to André."

"So says the one who wants to be his daughter."

Rebekkah frowned. "If you aren't going to be civil today, then I suggest you find someone else to work with for awhile."

Michael sighed. "I didn't mean it, Rebekkah. It's frustrating. But I suppose that doesn't matter. You probably have no idea what it's like to grow up like I did." With a shrug he turned and headed toward the elevators. "I'll get that information for you."

As Rebekkah watched him walk off, she thought about what he said and wondered what he'd do if she told him he was wrong, dead wrong about how she'd grown up.

She knew only too well what it was like to grow up in a single-parent household where the one parent had too many other things to think about than a child to raise.

But telling him that would do no good. Michael was caught up in a one-man pity party, and it was going to take more than her words to heal him.

Once in her office, she sat down at her desk and pulled out her Bible. Taking a deep breath, she worked to calm herself and began reading.

It was true what the Bible said, that God would take care of the problems and make them shine like the noonday sun. She loved Psalms, and as she read, she thought that was what was going to have to happen with the Watson family. God was going to have to somehow intervene and keep this dysfunctional, hurting family from completely self-destructing.

"Father, please help them. And help me help them, too. Especially André. He's so much like his father." She paused and rubbed a hand over her burning eyes. *"They just need to see the other one cares. If they could only see that..."*

She thought of her mother, in the apartment downtown, in a place she hadn't been back to in three years, and admitted, "If I can't take care of my own family, who am I to interfere in this one?"

She had a feeling, however, that maybe through this family she was going to find the peace she was seeking. She wasn't sure how, but she was sure God was in control, and that in every single thing she got involved in, God would somehow show His glory and teach her.

And she wanted to be taught, except in the one area—the very area it seemed she was headed—families.

"I don't understand why they all seem to trust me, Father, but help me to understand. Help me, Father, to be what You want me to be and guide me, Father, as I try to help Drydan find the peace with his son he is searching for."

Turning to her Bible to read a bit more before returning to work, Rebekkah admitted it was going to be a long day.

Chapter Six

"I'm glad you could have lunch with me," André said to Sarah and Justin as they seated themselves. "How's the pregnancy going?"

André couldn't miss how wide Sarah had grown around the middle since he'd last seen her. Willowy, blond, quiet and sweet, Sarah had been the love of his life—until his father had fired her.

No, that wasn't accurate. He and Sarah had floated into a relationship, from working together to dating and then deciding it was the right thing to do. He had wanted a family, someone to start teaching about the business and to follow in his footsteps one day. Sarah had always seemed like the perfect woman. Especially since his father had insisted that she might not be. Drydan didn't like that she came from poverty, or so André had thought.

It wasn't until they'd found out Sarah was infertile and he'd left on business for time to think about what Sarah had said that he'd questioned if they were really right for each other. He had decided they could adopt— without consulting Sarah.

When he'd returned, he'd found her gone, fired and living with her former brother-in-law as a housekeeper and nanny to his five-year-old daughter, Mickie.

Justin, her former brother-in-law and now husband, groaned. "Appetite? Let me tell you what type of appetite this woman has. She's eating us out of house and home in tacos."

Sarah elbowed her husband. "Enough, potbelly," she warned, poking at her husband's flat midriff.

"Potbelly?"

"She enjoys calling me that even though I don't have one." Justin shrugged.

André smiled, his eyes twinkling. "Sarah, I don't remember you having a Mexican food craving."

Sarah eased her body into the chair opposite André. Justin sat down next to her. "I didn't. Not until a few weeks ago when I finally started keeping food down."

"Nearly five months," Justin muttered.

André remembered Sarah had been having trouble with that for the past few months—over half her pregnancy. "Did it stop on its own or did the doctor intervene?" he asked, concerned.

Justin reached over and took his wife's hand. A tender smile on his face, he remarked, "God intervened. Nothing was helping until we went up for prayer."

"That's right," Sarah added softly.

André watched Sarah's features turn soft and sweet as she gazed at her husband.

"And Mickie?" André asked about Justin's daughter and Sarah's stepdaughter and niece. She hadn't seen her niece in nearly three years, if he remembered correctly, since she'd tried to take the child from Justin in a nasty court battle. She hadn't seen Justin, either.

But hearing Justin needed a housekeeper and her being out of money from what André's father had done, Sarah had turned to her brother-in-law for help.

And he had helped her—both of them falling in love in the process.

"She's growing. She's almost eight, as she likes to remind us. She will be in a few days." Sarah chuckled and rolled her eyes.

"Motherhood has done you good, Sarah."

Sarah shifted uncomfortably, her glance going from André to Justin and back. He knew what she was thinking. Because the doctor had said she most likely wouldn't have children, the two of them had broken up, and now here she was with child.

Somehow he found that didn't bother him, however. As a matter of fact, watching the two interact had hurt him at first. Now, sitting here, he wasn't sure what had changed, but he realized he only wished them the best.

He'd long ago accepted their union. Now there was no more hurt or frustration or any lingering romantic feelings.

Justin squeezed his wife's hand before releasing it, and André realized he was happy for the two of them.

The waitress approached, stopping conversation, and they all ordered salads—Sarah a taco salad, to which they laughed.

When all quieted down, Sarah asked, "So what is this again about the Kittering case?"

André quickly explained. "It seems, going back over what I remember, that they claim they didn't know anything about a lawsuit and were found innocent of what had been brought against them. New evidence tends to suggest there was a big cover-up. Word has it that the case is being appealed and it might just affect my father and his business. Dad checked into it, and sure enough, rumors are someone is getting ready to okay the appeal and set a date." He ended by saying, "So, I wanted to know if you might have private notes stored somewhere on the case? I'm gathering anything I might be able to find while Rebekkah is collecting all the old records. All information will help at this point, since we didn't ever expect an appeal out of this.''

Sarah frowned. ''I don't remember taking anything with me when I left. If I did have private records of anything, they'd be in a box in the archives, most likely.''

The salads and drinks arrived as he pondered her words.

Justin asked, ''Mind if we pray?''

André nodded and bowed his head.

When the prayer ended they started eating. ''I am thinking, perhaps, since you kept such thorough notes, we might find something in there. I'll have Rebekkah check.''

''Are you working with your dad again?'' Sarah asked softly.

''Honey,'' Justin said, with a warning tone.

''No, it's all right.'' André sighed. ''I am sorry, Sarah, for what happened with you, and I know you say you forgive him, but I can't. I want to hear him say he was wrong before I do.''

"That's not a good attitude to have," Sarah said as she continued to eat.

"That's just how I feel."

"Why?" Justin asked as André took a bite.

André glanced at the quiet man by Sarah's side. Surprised, he said, "I loved her and—"

"Do you still love her?" Justin asked bluntly.

"Justin! You promised," Sarah said, shock in her voice.

"No, Sarah. André and I have danced around this for two years. I've accepted him as friend. I think this is something that is long overdue."

"He's right, Sarah," André said, studying Justin.

"Men," Sarah muttered. "I should have known you were up to something when you agreed to come on such short notice, Justin."

She scowled, which made both men grin.

Justin's sharp gaze was on André though, even as he grinned. André realized this was something that hung between them. How did he feel about Sarah?

Glancing from her to Justin, he admitted, "It's obvious you are both deeply in love."

Sarah reached out for André's hand and squeezed it. He squeezed back and then released it. "It's all right, Sarah. I think, believe it or not, I've always cared deeply for you, but I do not think it was love, looking back on it."

Sarah looked relieved while Justin looked pleased.

"Justin shouldn't have put you on the spot," Sarah said, giving her husband a fierce look.

"If you were my woman—"

"Which she's not," Justin interrupted.

"Which she's not," André confirmed wryly, "I think I would have asked long before now. Especially if the man kept coming around. I suppose that should tell us something right there. Had I loved you as deeply as Justin does, I don't think I would have been able to come around while you were married to another man."

"Oh, André," Sarah said, and started crying.

"Sarah?" André leaned forward, worried. She waved him off.

"She's been doing this since she got pregnant," Justin said.

André admitted he had seen her cry two other times, but...

"I'm happy," she muttered and sniffled loudly before pulling up her napkin to dab at her eyes. She looked so cute in the large polka-dot blue and white top and blue skirt with her blond hair pulled up in a long ponytail. He couldn't help but smile.

"I think I'm glad, at the moment, I'm single," André said.

She threw her napkin at him.

He chuckled.

"I'm glad she's not," Justin murmured fervently.

"Me, too," Sarah replied, smiling at her husband, tears forgotten.

Shaking his head, André thought he'd never understand the relationship between the two.

Sarah finally turned from her husband to meet André's gaze. "So if I forgive your father and you don't love me, André, why are you still holding a grudge against your father?"

André's smile collapsed into a scowl. "She's your wife. Tell her I don't have to have a reason."

"Uh-uh," Justin said, shaking his head. Leaning back, he continued, "I agree with Sarah. Your father has changed in the last two years. Word in the community is he's cleaning up his act."

André shrugged. "I have my own company now."

"We know that, but you did say you were working on this case with Rebekkah, so I thought you might have..." Sarah paused and lifted her hands in a shrug.

"No. If he will admit he is wrong, then we can go on from there. He is stubborn, and what he did was wrong. I'm tired of him controlling my life."

"You're both stubborn, André," Sarah said.

André stiffened.

"So are you, my dear," Justin said lightly.

She gasped. "I am not."

André chuckled.

"Don't you agree," Sarah warned.

André lifted both hands. "Don't worry. I know better."

They all laughed.

"You know, André," Sarah said as they finished their salads, "bitterness will eat away at you. Even if you believe God has led you to the inner city, you started that career in bitterness, and it's not going to have a good foundation if you don't forgive your father."

André scowled. "He doesn't really care about me, Sarah. It's control he wants."

Slowly, Sarah shook her head. "I don't think so. I've heard he doesn't even know you're going to that inner-city church on Wednesday nights and some Sundays. He thinks you've dropped out."

"We don't talk." André pushed his plate back and dabbed at his mouth with his napkin.

"Holding a grudge isn't a good thing, man," Justin said. "Believe me. It almost ruined Sarah's life, not to mention mine."

André knew that Justin had forbidden Sarah to come around Mickie ever again after their court battle and understood the strife that had caused. "If I could believe my father really cared and this wasn't some new manipulation to control my life..." André shook his head. "Why have something happen again? No, Sarah, I think God will just have to intervene in this."

It was Justin's turn to shake his head. "He did on the cross when He took our sins, André. If He can forgive, what right do we have not to forgive?"

André sighed. "I'm not ready."

"I won't say anything more, friend," Sarah said. "Except God tells us not to let the sun go down on our wrath. You need to work it out. What would you do if your father died before you had a chance to forgive each other? Please just think about that."

"I will, Sarah," André muttered, glad to have her promise to lay off. Every time they got together, which wasn't often, since he had been avoiding her since he'd heard of the pregnancy, eventually she brought up forgiving his father. How she could forgive him, he didn't know.

If his father would admit he was wrong or somehow show André that he really wasn't just trying to control him again—that would be the difference.

"How's Rebekkah working out there?" Sarah asked.

"Good. Really good. I have to say I'm very impressed with her. Though my father hired her originally to fill an extra slot, she's now one of his more trusted advisers and handles some of his hardest cases. Unfortunately, she's fallen for that charisma he has, hook, line and sinker. She dotes on his every word—even having dinner with him and Mom occasionally."

"I knew her career had taken off, but that's great," Justin said. "I had no idea she'd grown so close to your father."

"She treats him like a long-lost relative." André shook his head. "I don't understand it at all."

"Maybe she's never had parents. Do you know her story?" Sarah asked.

André realized he didn't. He had no idea if she had a mom or dad, if she had come from out of state. He had no idea about anything before she'd started working for his dad, except she'd graduated top of her class from law school in Louisiana.

"I guess I don't," he murmured.

Sarah happened to glance at her watch. "We have to get Mickie," she told Justin. "She's getting out early today."

André glanced at his watch. "And I have a two o'clock appointment I don't want to miss. Thank you again for having lunch." André pulled out some money and tossed it on the table, enough to cover all their meals. When Justin started to object, André said, "You can treat me next time. Gotta go." He stood and strode off before they could argue.

Sarah looked good. She was happy, pregnant and growing in all kinds of ways that he hadn't imagined for her. He was happy for her. Justin was happy, too, he thought as he left the café and strode toward his car.

Where had his life gone the past few years? It seemed only yesterday that he'd broken up with Sarah and yet, sitting there at lunch, it had seemed like another lifetime.

He'd been drifting, wading in hurt and what ifs, he realized. That and building up a business, ignoring the world around him.

He realized his ignorance when Sarah had asked him about Rebekkah. She had been hired just before he'd left the company. Yet, what did he know about her? He'd talked with her several times, even sparred with her, yet he really didn't know much more about her than he had the day she was hired.

Had he been so caught up in other things that he didn't even notice the person on the corner or down the hall from him?

Life was passing him by. Sarah and Justin's love was proof of that. They had grown and developed while it seemed like he'd stopped living.

Well, it was time to start again.

Realizing he had stopped in front of his car and stood there, he unlocked the door and slid in.

After buckling up, he started the car and headed toward his office.

It was definitely time to start living again. He might have issues he wanted to deal with, but that wouldn't stop him from seeking direction for his life. And one thing he was going to do was find out about Rebekkah Hawkley.

Tonight.

Chapter Seven

He'd seen the attraction and thought André could hold his own. How long did it take for the man to make a move?

He had lost respect for André. Had he had Rebekkah at his beck and call, the woman wouldn't have her car piled high with documents like she did right now.

Pulling down the black mask, he stared into the darkened car, glad the light was out where she had parked. It made it so much easier for him to do his job.

A job he wouldn't necessarily enjoy. But a job that had to be performed just the same.

After all, it was André he sought to quiet, and Rebekkah Hawkley was simply in the way of that. If André was off the case then his partner wouldn't be on the case, as well.

It all boiled down to taking care of André's need to find the proof.

Pulling out a can of gasoline, he thought it a shame what he was about to do.

Church went wonderfully, as far as Rebekkah was concerned. She enjoyed the service and was glad to have company to sit with that evening. She often found herself sitting alone on Wednesday nights.

As they got up to go, André slipped a hand to her back to escort her out. She liked the warmth of that hand there. There was no doubt about it. She could deny it all she wanted to, but the simple fact was, she was physically attracted to this man, and finding out as they chatted that she liked his personality, too. If only he could solve some of his problems, she thought, and then was pricked in her conscience as she admitted she had a few of her own that needed solving. "So, what did you think of the service?'' she asked as they walked down the aisle and into the foyer.

"Other than he preached constantly on forgiving trespasses?'' André said wryly. "I would think you put the preacher up to that if I didn't know better.''

Rebekkah grinned. "Hey, his sermon touched my heart, as well.''

She nodded to those she knew as they exited the building. "You can follow me home if you'd like.'' She missed his hand at her back as he moved it to fish for his keys.

"Where did you park?'' André asked. He waited expectantly.

"This way,'' Rebekkah replied. "And you?''

He nodded in the same direction she'd indicated. Together they started across the parking lot. Rebekkah had been running late and was parked pretty far back in the asphalted area, where the lighting wasn't good. Normally she didn't park in a place like that, but in a church parking lot, all should be fine, she thought.

Until she saw something.

The hairs on the back of her neck stood up. "Was that..." She thought she saw a shadow near her car, but surely not. "Did you see that?"

"What?" André asked, pausing, his hand instinctively going to her back and spreading in a comforting gesture.

"Out there, by my car." She pointed.

André squinted. "You shouldn't park in a place like that—"

Exasperated, Rebekkah cut him off. "I was running late. It was one of the few places left. Normally I don't park somewhere like that. Look there!" She pointed.

Just as she did, her entire car went up in flames.

"Oh, my gosh..." Stunned, she stood there, still pointing, certain she wasn't seeing what she was seeing.

"Fire! Someone's car is on fire!"

Galvanized by the shouts, she sprinted forward, only to be abruptly halted by André as he pulled her into the frame of his body. "No!"

"My car!" she cried, and wiggled to get free.

"Someone call the fire department!" André shouted.

Rebekkah jerked again. "I need to—"

"To what?" André asked. "You saw someone. I saw someone, too. It's obviously arson, and we aren't taking chances the person who started it is still out there."

"Arson?" Rebekkah's mind was slow but still functioning. It dawned on her suddenly what she had seen. "Someone set that blaze."

"You got it in one, counselor," André muttered, continuing to hold her tightly against him as he stared over her shoulder toward the car.

Aware of the proximity, she leaned into him, allowing his voice next to her ear to comfort her—as much as she could be comforted in this instance.

Someone had grabbed a fire extinguisher, but Rebekkah could smell the fuel from here. Another person had a water hose but didn't approach. Everyone knew it was a loss. People who had parked nearby were lamenting the danger to their cars, but no one went forward.

Sirens sounded in the distance.

"Why?"

"Do you know anyone who would do that?" André asked quietly.

Sadly she shook her head. "I'd just finished paying it off."

"A random act of violence, then." André loosened his hold and rubbed his hands up and down her arms in comfort.

"Why me?"

Turning her, he pulled her into his arms and hugged her. "Random, Bekka. That means exactly that. You weren't targeted, it was just luck. The youth pastor here has been doing a lot of work with gangs. It's possible some gang leader didn't like the fact the youth pastor had been on his case and wanted to make a statement to the church in general. Wait for the police to get here, and the firemen. I'll give you a ride home. It'll be okay."

Rebekkah inched her hands up until she

clung to him, resting in his warmth as her numbed mind tried to process that someone had blindly struck out in anger and attacked her personal property.

"Were the records in there?" André asked, resigned.

"Records?"

Then she realized what he was asking. A glimmer of light shone in the dark tunnel of despair. "Well, the good news is I had all except the loose reports out of the car. For that case, at least. Another case I had in there, though."

"Really? Well, there is that, at least—that it wasn't everything, that is." Squeezing her arms, he stepped back until he could see into her gaze. "How about some more good news?"

"What's that? My car is toasting to its death as we speak, and I hate car hunting and…" She trailed off.

He grinned. "Hmm…how about this. Would it be good news if I said I'll go out car hunting with you tomorrow and we can spend the day off work?"

Rebekkah chuckled. "That's good news? I just said I hate car hunting."

"I'm offended," André teased, straightening as if affronted. "I don't offer to go car hunting with just anyone."

Rebekkah looked up at André at the change in him, to see what he was up to. His eyes twinkled as he grinned. She realized he was trying to cheer her. "And just who do you go car hunting with?" she queried, playing along to see where this was going.

"Only people who've had car fires."

"You know many, do you?" she asked wryly, the shock of losing her car receding in the light of André's silly antics.

"In my line of business?" The you've-got-to-be-kidding look on his face did her in.

She burst into laughter. "You got me there. In our line, I guess we do!"

The sirens grew steadily louder then ceased as fire trucks followed by police cars pulled into the parking lot.

André slipped an arm around Rebekkah and escorted her toward the police cars. The firemen hurriedly put out the fire and doused the vehicles around hers, which looked singed but none the worse for wear.

A police officer took their report, and others, as well, and then André escorted her to his car. He drove her home.

"I appreciate you bringing me home like this, André," Rebekkah said as they pulled into the apartment complex where she lived.

"No problem. I did have to come back and look at some of those reports."

She nodded. After swinging her legs out of the sleek black midsize car he owned, she grabbed her purse and shut the door. Then together they climbed the stairs to her second-story apartment.

"A nice place here. Not much crime," André commented as they paused outside her door while she slipped the key into the lock.

"That's why I chose it. Fenced in all around, older people living here with families rather than singles, except for this area right here, which is single dwellings. I don't have to worry about solicitors since they're not allowed. And the management takes care of everything."

She flipped the light on as she entered. André glanced around the room, finding it impressive but nearly empty of warmth. A standard sofa and chair that looked rarely used with a TV and stereo sat in the living room. To the left was a kitchen, tiny but just the right size for one or two people.

A collection of elephant statues was on display across a shelf between the two areas right by the hall entrance.

Three doors, one most likely a bathroom, another a bedroom, and he'd bet the last one was a utility room since a basket sat next to the shutter-type folding doors.

The only personal touch he saw was a photograph of a young woman with a baby on her hip. The tiny shack behind them looked very run-down and very poor. Interesting, André thought. "You and your mom?"

Rebekkah glanced over her shoulder. An indescribable look crossed her face. "That was a long time ago."

"Oh. She's dead?" he asked, and started to apologize when she shook her head.

"She's still alive."

André trying to cover the awkwardness he felt, said, "You should update your pictures."

Pulling out boxes from behind a small alcove in the kitchen, she again shook her head. "I prefer that memory to later ones."

André hurried to her side and assisted her in getting the several boxes on the table. Realizing it best not to ask any more questions, he told himself to be the gentleman.

But as she stood to face him, he couldn't help but add, "You grew up poor, didn't you?"

Rebekkah's lips thinned, and she nodded. "Have a seat."

Seating herself at the linoleum table, she pulled off the lids of each box, She took out an inventory sheet from the boxes and stacked them together.

André accepted the subject was closed— for now. He wanted to know more about the woman who held the child with the huge grin on her face.

"Michael and a colleague made sure all

these got to my car.'' She hesitated then continued. ''They're everything they could dig up on the case.''

''I didn't know we'd generated that much paperwork,'' he murmured.

''Yeah, it's a lot. If we split it, we might make faster progress and actually find something. I scanned some of it before church tonight, and there are a lot of places referred to in Alaska that I don't know.''

''I went up there when the case first opened. The owner was a friend of my mom's and wanted us to handle the case. So they got first-class treatment, which meant us making regular trips up there.''

''Friendly with them?''

''They've given us a lot of business over the years,'' André confirmed.

''So, which boxes do you want?''

André glanced at Rebekkah. She sat, hands resting on the box in front of her, staring at him. ''How about we work here each night instead of dragging them back and forth? Who knows, there might be something cross-referenced to one of these.''

The idea had come to him as he'd stared at her. Keep everything here, and he might just find out more about this woman.

Rebekkah grimaced. "Unfortunately, that makes sense."

André smiled. He was glad, because it didn't to him. He wasn't going to get much work done with her sitting across the table from him.

He didn't plan to tell her that, however. Nor did he plan to tell her that he enjoyed her company and was curious about her.

"Did your mom call you Bekka?" he asked now.

Rebekkah let out a frustrated sigh. "You aren't going to let it go, are you?"

"What's that?"

"Poking and prodding. I should have hidden the picture before you came over," she muttered.

"But then I wouldn't have been able to poke and prod to find out more."

Pushing a box aside, he crossed his arms on the table. "This can wait a minute. I'm still trying to figure out your reaction earlier to when I called you Bekka. You didn't flinch. It must be a regular endearment.''

Rebekkah threw her hands in the air. "If I go over this, will we get back to work?''

Seeing her agitated amused him. Her cheeks darkened, eyes narrowed, but somehow he knew it wasn't from anger but sheer nervousness. He should stop now, but...

"I promise," he said quietly.

She clasped her hands in front of her. "I am from a single-parent household. I'm sure, with your keen perceptions, you noted the house behind my mom and me. At that time I was young and didn't understand the different uncles that visited Mom. Mom was happy, and most of the time an uncle lasted a long time. But as she grew older and I grew older, things changed.

"I was determined to get away from that life. An inner-city bus ministry that came through on Saturdays picked me up one Saturday, and I gladly went. That was when I found God.''

Her features softened. "I had no idea there was a God up there Who cared for me.

Feeling betrayed as I did, by Mom, by those men who came by…'' Shaking her head, she continued. ''I thought Mom would be excited. And she was, for me…but I've never been able to get her to attend church with me, or to make a commitment to Christ.''

Rebekkah's hands clenched. ''When I couldn't stand it any longer I vowed to get out. And I did. And I don't plan on going back—ever.''

André frowned. ''Do you go see your mom?''

A short nod answered his question. ''On holidays mostly.''

André wanted to thank her for being honest. Instead, he said, ''I used to be driven to school every day. Only the best for André.'' With a wry smile he continued. ''You can imagine how that went over with the school kids in the area. Private school. Private parties with only the elite invited to the birthday parties.

''We attended church, but my dad wasn't a Christian. It was a social thing. You were supposed to go on Sunday morning and dress up, like a family should. I got saved one Sunday in church. My dad couldn't understand why I wanted to go on Sunday night or Wednesday or to any other functions. A lot of the times he forbade me because there were other more important things to do.''

Rebekkah nodded, listening. André remembered those times with bitterness. ''I backslid. I got interested in the business and decided that was my destiny. I pushed hard, devoting all of my time to it, planning to be the next Kennedy. I found the perfect wife. She'd make a good hostess, and we enjoyed each other's company. She wasn't what my dad wanted, which was a bit pleasing.'' He offered Rebekkah a smile. ''Then I lost her, and my life turned upside down.''

''Your dad is sorry,'' Rebekkah murmured.

''No.'' André sat back. ''Don't defend him to me, Rebekkah. I'm just telling you where I come from. The way you shared with me. Maybe you can see why I am not too interested in the business now.''

"What about your anger at your father? Is that a reason, as well?"

André shrugged. "Yeah. And I know I have to forgive him, but it's the how... I just can't find a way to make myself."

Rebekkah nodded, as if in contemplation.

"I think, perhaps, Bekka," André said slowly, "that we have that in common, do we not?"

Rebekkah glanced at the small decorative picture frame on the side table that held the picture of her and her mom.

That was answer enough for André. He said, "I guess you were right. That sermon tonight was for both of us. You pray for me, Rebekkah, and I'll pray for you, and we'll believe that God can bring a reconciliation about. How's that?"

Rebekkah nodded. "Better be careful what you pray for, André."

André smiled. "Oh, I am. Believe me. I am."

And he was certain he was going to be praying God help him find more time to spend around this woman.

"Now back to work?" Rebekkah asked, definitely more relaxed, as if a wall had been knocked down between them with the fact that they now knew a bit more about each other.

"Back to work," he murmured and sat there for the next three hours reading reports and listening to the sharp, concise suggestions of the next upcoming star of Watson and Watson.

Chapter Eight

"Are you sure this is the car you want?"

"Yes." Rebekkah stuck her hands in her jacket pockets and glared at André.

"You've said that at the last three car lots."

"And you've insisted on checking out one more each time," she accused.

"You can't just walk onto a lot and point to a car and buy it. You need to examine, compare, test drive."

Annoyed, she again asked, "Why?"

André ran a hand through his perfect hair. Which pleased Rebekkah and eased her frustration. He was driving her crazy, car shopping, and it was nice to see she had ruffled his feathers—or hair, as the case might be.

"This is an investment, something you're going to be stuck with awhile. What if you don't like it?"

"It has four wheels. It's new. It's cheap. I like it."

The salesman smiled and started to suggest something, but André lifted a hand. "Let me leave a credit card and we can drive it for the day. If you like it, then you can buy it. How's that?"

"For the day?" Rebekkah glanced from André to the salesman and back. "Is that legal?"

"Yes, ma'am," the salesman said and handed André the keys.

André reached in his pocket, pulled out one of his platinum cards and gave it to the salesman.

Rebekkah glared and snatched the keys from André. "I'm the one buying it, not you. And maybe I don't want to do this."

"If you do, I promise you we won't go to another car lot."

"Run his card," she said, turning to the salesman.

"Oh, no. No. I don't have to run Mr. Watson's card. This is fine. Fine."

She hated small towns, she decided, listening to the salesman fawn over André.

"You two take the car and run whatever errands you want. I'll just do the paperwork and we'll have it ready when you come back, in case you're interested."

"It's for me. Not him," Rebekkah said.

"Of course, Ms. Hawkley. Have fun."

"Let's go," André said.

"You're going with me?" she asked as André started her toward the compact foreign car she'd pointed to earlier.

"I'll help you test drive it. Besides, I have a friend I'd like you to meet. Why take two cars when we can take one instead? And if you don't like it, then I need to be able to take you somewhere else."

Rebekkah groaned. "I am going to buy it. I promise. I hate car shopping."

André pulled the door open for her, and she slid in behind the wheel.

He walked to the passenger's side and got in.

Rebekkah burst into laughter.

André's knees were at his chest.

A crooked grin on his face, he said, "At least you're smiling now." Feeling around, he found the release and slid the seat back. "I don't know that I've ever been in a car this size."

"It's all I can afford right now," she retorted. "And it's the one I'm going to buy. So if you plan on ever riding anywhere with me you'll get used to it now."

André grinned.

She melted. So much for being upset at him. When he'd shown up this morning she'd thought it would take thirty minutes. Go to the car place a few miles away and sign some paperwork.

But no. André insisted she look somewhere else before she buy. When she'd pointed to a car, he'd grown suspicious and decided she had to check out another place. He'd brought her to another place, and as soon as she'd pointed he'd put her back in the car and driven off.

All the way here he'd explained she had to take time, pick out a car that would fit her, one that would be exactly what she wanted—not simply the first choice.

So she'd pretended to look around when she'd gotten here, walking from car to car, and then she'd pointed.

Which had brought her to where she was now.

"Are all men like you?"

"What do you mean?" André asked as she started the car.

"Insisting on going from place to place to place."

"That's a woman thing."

"Not this woman," she muttered.

"Exactly, which had me worried."

"If you turn sexist on me..."

"Not me," André said. Buckling himself up, he waved a hand in the air. "Go down this street and I'll show you where to go. I want you to chat with Sarah. I promised to come by today and pick up some notes she'd made about the case we're researching—just things she's remembered, but they might help."

"Don't forget. You said no more car hunting if I drove this car."

André nodded and directed her to Sarah's. "I agree. So tell me," he drawled as she turned left onto the main street. "Did you think about me last night?"

She overshot the lane.

André grinned, making her want to smack him.

"No. I did *not* think about you last night."

His grin spread. "I thought about you, Bekka. Do you know what I realized last night?"

Scowling she said, "No. I'm not a mind reader."

"I realized you are quite a fun person to be around."

Despite her scowl she was certain her heart skipped a beat. He enjoyed her company. Now that was interesting. "I can be a crab, as well."

André chuckled, sending tingles up her spine. "Yeah, well...maybe I like seafood."

She rolled her eyes and then turned onto

the side road André directed her to. "I'm allergic. Horribly."

"Liar."

She remembered eating seafood with him the other night. Deciding a tactical maneuver was in order, she said, "This car drives really well. What do you think?"

Out of the corner of her eye she saw the smug smile he wore. He thought he'd gotten under her skin.

Okay, so he had, but it was only temporary. He wasn't going to like it that she wanted him to forgive his father. He wasn't going to like it that she considered his father the father she never had.

That would cause problems if they tried to enter into a relationship.

But she liked this man.

She'd have to be confident that André was going to forgive his father and they would be able to date and not kill each other over the subject.

Wishful thinking.

"To the right."

"Huh?" Glancing at him, she realized

there was the street she was supposed to turn on. Quickly she executed a turn that had André gripping the chicken bar over the passenger door. "You, uh, like to express yourself behind the wheel, don't you?"

It was her turn to smile. "Yeah, I do. Now what were you saying?"

"I was saying that the car might be a tad out of alignment, but I take that back. I think that was your driving, not the car."

Rebekkah relaxed, grinning. "Don't like my driving, huh?"

André tried to look polite, but she caught the grimace.

She chuckled. "And just think, you are going to be with me *all* day as I test drive." At the driveway of the house they were going to, she executed a sharp, fast turn, hitting the gas and then braking as soon as they got into it.

André gave her a very long-suffering look and released his seat belt. "I see, counselor, that telling you anything is dangerous. You'll use it against me at your first chance."

After pulling the key from the ignition, she exited the car. She grabbed her purse, dropped the key in, closed the door, then rounded the hood. "You got it in one, counselor," she retorted.

Together they went up the cement walk to the flower-lined porch.

André rang the doorbell.

Inside they heard noise, then a chain sliding. When Sarah pulled open the door, Rebekkah noted that Sarah had certainly grown since the last time she'd seen her. She thought she was only three or four months pregnant. She looked as if she were ready to drop the baby any day!

"André! Rebekkah. Come in. I doubt you remember me, Rebekkah. I used to be—"

"I know you. I've seen you around town, as well. Nice to see you again." Rebekkah stuck out her hand, and Sarah took it, squeezing it.

"Come in. I'm so glad you made it, André. I have eight pages of notes for you."

"Eight!" He couldn't hide his surprise.

Sarah blushed. "Well, like I said, I'm

glad you stopped by. The more I thought about it, the more little things came back to me. Come on in.''

Sarah turned and crossed the living room to the kitchen. Rebekkah and André went into the living room, where they waited.

It was a nice house, big front window, fireplace, sofa with a coffee table that had a picture book on it.

In the corner she saw a basket with dolls and homemade clothes. Above the fireplace mantel hung a family portrait, very recent. Sarah was pregnant, though not as big as now. Her husband stood proudly next to her, and in front of them was a seven-year-old child, hair caught to the side in a ponytail that lay across her shoulder. The ends of the hair hung just past her shoulder, a scrunchy holder keeping it neat.

Above the mantel was a woman who looked similar to Sarah, most likely a sister, and pictures of Mickie as a baby.

A home, Rebekkah thought longingly. Not just a house, but also a home.

"That's Sarah's sister. At one time her

sister and Sarah's husband were married—before she died," André informed her.

Before she could reply, Sarah was back. "Oh, you should have sat down. I'm sorry. Would you like something to drink?"

Sarah seated herself in a rocking chair. André motioned Rebekkah forward, and they both sat.

"Not for me, thank you," Rebekkah murmured.

"No, thanks, Sarah." André looked perfectly relaxed sitting on the sofa, one ankle crossed over a knee.

"So what brought you by in that car?" Sarah asked, quickly scanning the notes before slipping them into a manila folder and passing it to André.

"We're car shopping. Someone torched Rebekkah's car last night, and she needs a new one."

"That's awful! Was it case related? Or maybe…"

Rebekkah calmed Sarah. "No. I didn't recognize the person."

"It *was* pitch black out," André murmured.

Rebekkah rolled her eyes. "I couldn't see the person but I'm not working on any volatile cases at the moment. The police are thinking it was just a random act of violence."

Sarah nodded. "There sure is a lot of that around."

"In the end days," Rebekkah murmured, "they say things are going to get worse and worse."

"That's true. So, you're test driving it?" Sarah asked.

Rebekkah scowled.

"Yes. She is," André replied.

"Yes," Rebekkah agreed.

Sarah's gaze went from one to the other. "André are you walking all over this poor woman?"

"Me?" André looked truly astonished.

Sarah tut-tutted at him. "He has a tendency to do his own thing. It's his way or no way, you'll discover, Rebekkah."

Rebekkah lifted an eyebrow, a slow smile curving her lips. "I've noticed that."

"Don't you two gang up on me," André protested. "That's not fair."

Sarah waved a hand in the air. "I've known you a long time. I know how you are. Take a firm hand with him, Rebekkah. Don't let him intimidate you."

Rebekkah chuckled. "He made me go to several different car places until I agreed to test this one."

"You couldn't find the one you wanted?"

"That wasn't the problem, Sarah," André replied. "Every single one we saw she tried to buy."

At Sarah's confused expression, Rebekkah elaborated. "I simply want a cheap, workable car, one that'll get me from point A to point B. Unfortunately, André here thinks we have to be choosy and try several before we buy."

Sarah's sweet laughter filled the room. "Oh, that's too much. I love it. Justin will die when he hears that. When we went car hunting it took me three months to find just what I wanted."

Rebekkah groaned. "Why so long?"

Sarah laid a hand on her stomach. "Well, it had to be the right size. This will be child number two in the family. And if we have another one in the next three or four years we'll need to make sure we have room for it, as well. And it had to be safe. I don't want my children in something dangerous.''

"Get a tank,'' André suggested.

Sarah giggled. "Same thing Justin said.''

"Now, that's not good.'' André frowned.

Rebekkah wondered if there was an old rivalry going here, if André had gotten over Sarah completely.

Sarah burst into laughter. "From what I understand, Justin got *that* idea from you!''

Well, maybe not, Rebekkah mused.

"I wanted to make sure about its test crashes and how much payments would be and that we get a good deal and...''

"I get the point,'' Rebekkah said, thinking if she went shopping with Sarah she'd pull her hair out.

"Do you like any type of shopping?'' Sarah asked Rebekkah.

Rebekkah thought about it. "Bath soaps. I like to walk through those stores.''

"Well, you'll get used to it if you decide

to have children. Do you like children?''
Sarah sat forward, studying Rebekkah
closely for the first time.

"Well...I guess so,'' Rebekkah replied.
"I've never thought much about it.''

"Never thought about having children?''
Sarah sounded as if Rebekkah had shocked
her down to her toes. "Forgive me, Rebekkah,'' she said. "It's just...'' Glancing at
André she nodded, and something passed
between them. Then she turned to Rebekkah. "I couldn't have children. Or at least,
I had been diagnosed infertile, according to
the doctors. That was what—well, anyway,
it was such a joy when a new procedure became available that helped me. I want to fill
the house now, though Justin isn't sure
about that.''

Again she laughed.

Rebekkah found Sarah's joy contagious
and realized she was smiling. "I guess if I
found the right man and settled down, eventually we'd have children. I suppose I'm just
so concentrated on my job right now that
I've never thought much about it.''

"That'll get you in trouble. Every woman—

and man, for that matter—that I've known who has concentrated solely on their career has ended up blindsided by love.''

''I don't think that's going to happen to me,'' Rebekkah replied, acutely aware that André sat next to her and hadn't said a word.

Sarah smiled a secret smile. ''You never know,'' she said.

André closed the manila folder and smiled at Sarah. ''Thank you for these notes. Now, leave poor Rebekkah alone. You're as bad as I am about teasing her.''

Turning, he smiled warmly at her, and Rebekkah felt herself relax. ''Sarah's pregnant. And happily married. She wants everyone else to be, as well.''

''I see,'' Rebekkah said.

André chuckled and stood. ''I'll go over these with Rebekkah more thoroughly later. If either one of us have a question, we'll call.''

Sarah pushed herself up out of the chair. ''Great. Thanks for stopping by.''

Rebekkah stood and squeezed the hand Sarah offered her, then walked out the front door.

Once they were in the car, Rebekkah asked, "Has she always been that exuberant?"

André shook his head. "Not until she met Justin. Love changed her."

Curiously, Rebekkah asked, "And you don't mind that?"

Holding her gaze, his steady and open for her to read the truth, he replied, "We would have been miserable together, because I was totally self-centered at that time. I am more than happy that she has found a man who can love her like she deserves, and I am very happy to call that man a friend. I realized the other day, when Justin asked, that I was well and truly over Sarah. What we had wasn't love but convenience, and I can assure you I'll never settle for that again. Not in love, and not in a job."

And that was that, Rebekkah thought. So much for bringing up his father.

She started the car, backed out and drove down the road to the car dealership thinking she'd just have to find a way to broach the subject later.

Chapter Nine

"**Y**ou haven't found out anything new?"

Rebekkah shifted in the leather chair, sighing in frustration. "No, and that's what bothers me. It seems to me since this firm represented Kittering we should have more on their parent company, but it's as if a huge part of it has just disappeared."

Drydan shook his head. "The split-up. When I bought out the other partners, several of the people who worked here left. Things were moved and archived. I imagine one of the former partners has some of the files, or they're sitting in our warehouse downtown."

"Which means it could likely take another two or three weeks to find anything. If it's okay with you, I'll go ahead and get Michael on it."

"How's he working out?" Drydan asked.

"Well," Rebekkah admitted, "he's a hard worker. A bit intimidated, I think, since André is back working on a case—"

"Understandable. He's new. He'll get over it. So, tell me about André."

Rebekkah, who had been thinking of him as well, glanced curiously at Drydan. "Yes?"

"Have you set up a dinner date yet?"

Had she? She had tried, several times, but something always seemed to get in the way. For a week now she'd been seeking a way to approach the thickheaded older son and get him to agree to a simple meal at his dad's. But at the mere mention of his dad's name, André closed up. "We've been so involved in the case…" She trailed off, knowing Drydan knew a half-truth when he heard one.

"Still that angry?" Drydan muttered.

"His business isn't doing as well as he'd want, but he has made progress since he's been out on his own. As long as that continues then he won't be coming back here."

Sighing, Rebekkah said patiently, "Being out on his own might be good for now, Drydan. Give it time."

"I'm just about out of time with him," he growled and shoved his chair back. He stood, then he strode across the room to the window. Hands clasped behind his back, he added, "I want him back, Rebekkah. I want this case solved. See what you can find and get me my son back."

She stood and crossed to him. "He's a grown man and makes his own decisions." At Drydan's frown, she added in a conciliatory tone, "But I'll see, Drydan. You both need to heal and get on with life, and that isn't going to happen until you two talk."

"Hmph."

She really hated it when Drydan was in this mood. Drawing on unseen strength, she continued, "If that's all…"

She didn't like reporting to Drydan about

the meetings she had with André. When he'd first suggested this, it had sounded reasonable. André was his son, and this was about the company. But as she'd gotten to know André and interact with him, she felt as if she were betraying him by reporting to Drydan. Today especially, since Drydan had played twenty questions with her.

"Yes, that's all." He waved a hand in dismissal, and gratefully she left.

As she started down the hall toward her office, Michael came up the stairwell. Seeing her, he turned toward her, waving a file. "I've found some more on that case you needed for tomorrow."

Rebekkah continued up the hall, taking the file from him and thumbing through it. "Thanks, Michael. That's great. Listen," she added, closing the file and slipping it under her arm. "The information you found for me on the Kittering case is great but incomplete."

"Yeah," Michael said, and followed Rebekkah into her office. "I couldn't find all of the files."

Rebekkah tossed the file on her desk, seated herself and pulled a piece of paper off the scrap pile.

"I talked with your father, and he suggests perhaps checking with the other partners and downtown in the archive building. What I'm looking for especially are memos from either company and memos we might have sent to them."

Michael perched on the desk. "Any reason why?"

Rebekkah rubbed the back of her neck and sighed. "It looks like the parent company knew about problems with Kittering and had them cover it up. Drydan needs to find out if this is true so we can do damage control. He also doesn't want to be involved with this company if they're going to drag him down with them."

"You think they'd do that?"

At the tone of Michael's voice, Rebekkah glanced up and studied him. "Either you are naive, Michael, or…"

"Or what?" Michael asked defensively. "I'm not so naive to think all companies are on the up-and-up."

Rebekkah shrugged. "I didn't mean anything by that." First Drydan being so touchy, and now Michael. Drydan was rubbing off on him. "At any rate." She shoved the paper at him. "Go see if you can locate any of these files. The partners' names and warehouse addresses are in the files here. I'll be working late tonight if you find anything."

"How late?"

Rebekkah shrugged. "Seven, most likely. I have a lot of work to catch up on for the case I have tomorrow, and then a bit more research for this problem, as well."

"You're working too hard, Rebekkah." Michael shook his head and folded the paper, slipping it into his pocket. "You need to be careful or you're going to burn yourself out."

Rebekkah disagreed. She thought of her goals, of making something of herself, and reasoned that this required hard work. "Sacrifice is part of becoming a success, Michael. Sometimes we have to do things we don't want to so we can reach our goals."

"Yeah," Michael murmured. Nodding, he stood and headed for the door. "Sometimes."

Rebekkah watched him go, wondering just what was on his mind. She knew he chafed over the fact that André had returned to help his father. She also had heard he'd grumbled about it to one of the secretaries down the hall.

Michael couldn't see that Drydan accepted him. What did Michael want? He had a good job, and Rebekkah knew Drydan had his eye on him for promotion. But if he didn't go to college, he couldn't do what his stepbrother did.

She wasn't sure it was a good idea for him to pursue a career as a lawyer. Honestly, Rebekkah thought that following a career in law might be a mistake for Michael. He was more free-spirited than his brother or father. She could picture Michael doing research for the company and enjoying the traveling that would go along with it.

He just had to get over this need to compete for his father's attention.

The sound of the phone interrupted her musings.

"This is Rebekkah," she said into the mouthpiece.

"Hey, Bekka." The sensual voice came over the line sending a warmth through her and bringing a smile to her face.

"Hello, André. How can I help you?" No way would she let him hear the pleasure his voice gave her.

"How's the car driving?"

"Just fine."

"Happy with your decision then?"

Resisting the urge to roll her eyes, she replied, "I would have been happy with the first car, or the second or the—"

His laughter cut her off. "Glad to know that."

Her lips curved in an answering grin. "So, what did you really call for? I'm sure you have better things to do than harass me over my car."

"I wanted to get together for dinner tonight if you have time."

"Dinner?" Rebekkah's heart fluttered,

though she hated to admit it. She didn't at all like the attraction she felt for this man. It was a distraction she could do without. Yet a part of her enjoyed it.

"Around six or so? I can make reservations for us."

"Um…" She hated to say no.

"Bad time?"

Sighing, she admitted, "I have some last-minute work I need to do for a case I have tomorrow and then I was going to work on our case some more. I didn't plan to leave here until around seven o'clock."

"That's fine. I can push back the reservations until then."

Relieved, she let out a breath. "Great. I'd like to go over some more questions on the case with you and information your father supplied, but this case tomorrow…"

"I know. I have a few other cases I'm working on, as well. Few as they are, I do have some business."

"I know that," Rebekkah answered gently. "I have one or two that are taking up my time right now that I couldn't lay aside to work solely on the Kittering case. I'm tying them up in the next couple of days, however, and then I can devote most of my time to this alone.''

''My dad is going to let you do that?''

''Don't sound so surprised. He's worried about the effect this is going to have on his business, as well as what might spill over onto you. He wants to get to the bottom of it as much as you do.''

''I suppose so.''

''Speaking of which...''

''Yeah?'' André asked, and she could hear the wariness that crept into his voice.

''I think we should have dinner with your parents sometime this week. We can go over everything about the case and—''

''I don't think so.''

Short and to the point, André cut her off. Frustrated, she replied, ''It might help the case.''

''Then you have dinner with them.''

''André!''

''I'm not ready for that Rebekkah,'' André said simply.

Rebekkah took a deep breath and let it out slowly. "Okay. Fine. I can understand that, but André, you are going to have to talk to your dad to find out how he's changed. It'd mean a lot to your mom."

It was André's turn to sigh with frustration. "He won't admit he was wrong."

"If you tried to make peace perhaps it'd make it easier for him to tell you."

"That's not how my dad works."

"What if he's changed, André?" she asked gently.

"What if your mom has changed?" André countered.

Rebekkah winced.

"I'm sorry." André sounded sincere over the phone, but it didn't help the pain she felt at his words.

"You're right. I shouldn't be casting stones when I can't get my own life in order," she replied, thinking about the fact she hadn't been home to her mom's in a long time.

"No, Rebekkah, I shouldn't have said that. Your situation is different. Yours could be dangerous. Please accept my apology."

Rebekkah wilted, the tension over his words seeping out of her. "Of course I do, André."

A short hesitation over the phone line told her he was unsure. Finally he asked, "Dinner still on?"

"I'd love to have dinner," she replied.

"How about we make our families off-limits for tonight and call a truce?" he asked.

Considering how off balance he kept her, she was more than happy to agree. "I'll be ready."

"Let me pick you up there, if that's okay. I'll be over in that area anyway."

"Sounds great," she replied, relaxing even more.

"See you then," he added, and his voice was back to the soft, sexy sound of earlier.

She couldn't help but respond with a warm smile. "I'll be here."

Hanging up the phone, she shook her head. She was in deep trouble with this guy. What was she going to do? She had her entire career in front of her and didn't have time for distractions. She was seriously considering allowing André to step into her life and probably change it in ways she couldn't even fathom.

Father, I'm not ready for this. There are too many things that need to be solved before I can even think about my emotions being involved. Look at the sparks he managed to pull up simply by mentioning my mom.

My mom. Rebekkah rubbed her temples. *I love her, Heavenly Father, I do, but…too much pain there. I don't want to go back.*

Rebekkah slumped despondently until a memory verse came to mind, Psalms 22, 5. *They cried unto Thee, and were delivered: they trusted in Thee, and were not confounded.*

It boiled down to simply trusting God, she realized. She had to believe things would work out right, not only with her mother, but with André as well. "You are in control, Heavenly Father," Rebekkah whispered. "Thank You for reminding me. How, Father, do I approach my mom after so many years? When? I just can't—yet."

But she knew, when the time was right, she'd be ready. She was afraid this situation with André and his father was God's way of preparing her to heal her own past.

Shaking her head, she admitted even when she didn't want what was best for her spiritually, God was merciful enough to see that she found it anyway.

And to see to that meant she was going to have to see André's heart healed first.

Which reminded her she'd better get busy if she was going to make the appointment with him tonight.

Chapter Ten

He'd thought she'd get the warning after the car.

It hadn't worked.

Angry, he paced. It was André he was after, but this woman was getting in the way.

He had to do something about her.

She hadn't given up on the case like he'd thought she would.

Of course, he should have checked in her car to make sure he was torching the right files.

Fisting his hands, he growled low in his throat, anger burning at the mistake.

They weren't going to win in this.

They couldn't.

If it meant teaching the woman a lesson to get her off the case then he'd do it.

But that case wasn't going to go any further.

No more information could be found.

It might have dire consequences if it was.

How to get the woman off the case?

As he paced and his anger increased, an idea formed.

After pulling the fax off the machine, Rebekkah examined it. The ringing of the phone had her crossing the room, paperwork in hand.

"Hello?"

"Are you still working?"

Rebekkah sat behind her desk and opened a briefcase. "I'm just finishing up, André. And I've found something interesting."

"About our case?"

"Yeah. I've traced some of the people this company talked with, and they gave me one name in particular. Supposedly it was a man who worked for the company that turned information over to us.''

''What type of information?''

Rebekkah hesitated.

André guessed. ''Memos?''

''You got it.''

''But we were defending the company,'' André argued. ''Besides, we never got anything like that. I would have remembered something that incriminated the business that used to be our meat and potatoes.''

Rebekkah could hear the frustration in André's voice. She couldn't blame him. ''I don't know if this information was falsified or not. It's possible someone's memory is faulty, or perhaps one of the people who wants to reopen the case is lying and forging documents. I'll put the memo I just got via fax in my briefcase, and you can examine it later.''

''Oh.'' André sounded as if he remembered something. ''I didn't think it possible, but your opening statement made me forget what I called for.''

Rebekkah finished filling her briefcase

and snapped it shut. "What was that?" she asked, a small smile playing about her lips.

"I happen to be about half a mile from your location."

The warm tones of his deep voice brought images of candlelight dinners. It was embarrassing how much she enjoyed this man's company. And how much she yearned for more with him. "I'd say that's perfect timing."

She enjoyed spending time with him and was glad things had worked out the way they had. "To be honest, I'll enjoy unwinding with you after a long day of work."

Perhaps she shouldn't have admitted that, but on the phone it seemed easier to be honest about her feelings. Doubt of course touched her when André didn't answer immediately. But before she could add anything he chuckled. "You have no idea the effect those words have on me, sweetheart, or you wouldn't say that."

A warm flush tingled through her body. Sweetheart.

"I'm glad to see my feelings aren't one-sided.'' In a soft, warm voice he continued, ''See you in five.''

Rebekkah hung up the phone. Hadn't she been worried not two hours earlier about the relationship being deeper than it had been?

So why had she purposely taken it another step forward?

''Because you've fallen for him, dingbat,'' she admonished herself. ''You've fallen hard and fast.''

Forcing herself to reality, she admitted André had a lot of problems and wasn't ready for a relationship right now. Nor was she. She had to come to terms with her past first—though she thought admitting that was a start.

She'd simply have to depend on God to help them work it out, because hormones weren't the only thing telling her this was the right guy for her.

She grabbed her briefcase, locked up and headed out of the office.

It had grown dark while she'd worked away the hours in her office. Dark and steamy, she thought with dismay as she exited the building. Taking a breath of the high humidity, she realized the reason it was so dark. Thick clouds had moved in that would soon bring rain. That was something they could always use, considering how dry this part of the state had been this summer.

But it still made it miserably sticky.

All was quiet as she glanced across the parking lot to her car. In the far distance she could hear traffic, but right here in the downtown area, there wasn't much noise except distant echoes. Most of the other office buildings had long been deserted, with normal employees going home by five in the evening.

Starting across the lot, she only heard the local sound of her low-heeled shoes clicking on the pavement.

She'd worked late a million times before, even in the dead of winter when it got dark as early as five o'clock. She'd always escorted herself to her car and driven home.

But as she walked across the parking lot to deposit her suit jacket in the car and wait for André, every hair on the back of her neck stood on end as if sensing some unseen danger.

Slowing her walk, she glanced around. But there was nothing to be seen.

She had to admit she'd been jumpy since someone had burned her car. Crime did that to a person, made them feel vulnerable.

But this was more than feeling exposed. This feeling was one of danger.

Coming to a stop, she studied her car. All the windows were still closed. She had locked it when she'd arrived today. No flat tires obvious. She could see nothing odd. No one was around it. It looked as if no one had tampered with it. There was no one out there.

Chills shivered down her back.

She knew, in her heart, something wasn't right. But what? She should have waited in the office until André got there. Then she wouldn't feel this way. She'd feel safe. It was stupid, but she knew what she was going to do. Although she'd been out on her own and had taken care of herself for years, she was going into the office to wait on an escort. She turned, intending to do just that.

And found what had made her so jumpy.

Coming toward her from around the corner of the office building was a man dressed in black with a mask over his face.

Gasping as her adrenaline jumped into gear, she whirled and started toward her car.

The man was on her before she'd taken two steps, knocking her to the ground.

Pain erupted at the weight that pinned her. Pain and pure fear. Her briefcase went flying as she landed on the pavement. She didn't take time to think but started clawing at the ground, trying to pull away from the man.

Strong arms slipped out and grabbed her wrists, pinning her to the ground. ''Leave well enough alone. He'll only cover it up again if you find out anything. They won't allow that.''

''What? I don't understand...''

''Drop it.'' The dark menacing voice so close to her ear could barely be heard over her pounding heart.

She had to escape. That's all her mind told her.

With a shove the man on top of her

pushed her into the unforgiving asphalt and then his weight left. The sound of running feet echoed even as headlights flashed into the parking lot, blinding her.

The squeal of tires and a door opening sounded beyond the light. "Rebekkah!"

"André!"

She rolled to her side and pushed at the ground to sit up.

"What happened? Are you okay?"

"D-did you see him?" Her teeth chattered as she asked the question. Her entire body began to tremble.

"Your hands are skinned, and your knees, sweetheart." Warm arms helped her into a sitting position and then slipped around her. "Repeat what you said?"

"Th-the man. Who-whoever m-mugged me."

"What!"

André released her to scope out the parking lot. Rebekkah cried out at the loss, bringing André's arms right back around her. "Shush, sweetheart. It's okay. The mugger is gone now. He probably saw me driving up."

Rebekkah curled her fingers into the lapels of André's jacket and buried her head in his chest, still trembling. His warmth, the strength of his arms around her were anchors in her suddenly unstable world.

"Let's get you inside." André shifted and picked her up, then quickly crossed the parking lot.

Realizing he couldn't reach his keys while holding her and knowing how silly she must look in his arms, she wiggled to get down.

André hesitated before releasing her. "Will you be okay standing on your own?"

The adrenaline rush had subsided. Rebekkah sagged against the glass next to the door. "I feel like I was just tackled by an NFL pro. My knees and hands along with my ribs think they've gone through the grinder, but yes, I'll be okay, André. I'm only glad..." She shuddered, realizing she wasn't as okay as she tried to put on, "I'm glad you showed up when you did."

André found his keys, unlocked the door, slipped an arm around Rebekkah and helped her into the foyer. He paused to lock the door behind them, then unlocked it. "I'll be right back." He strode across the parking lock, killed the engine of his car, grabbed her briefcase and returned.

Despite all that had just happened, Rebekkah chuckled. It was nervous energy being released, she supposed, since the adrenaline had no other way to bleed off.

"What's so funny?"

"I was just picturing you having to car hunt if your car was stolen."

André set the briefcase aside and strode to Rebekkah. Grabbing her upper arms, he pulled her to him. "Believe me, my car being stolen is the last thing on my mind right now." Locking eyes with her, he slowly lowered his head until their lips touched.

Sweet, gentle, yet filled with passion, his lips caressed her own. Rebekkah immediately responded, deepening the kiss. She could feel André's response as he pulled her closer, wrapping his arms around her.

Then he stiffened and set her back. "This is the wrong time. I'm sorry, honey."

Rubbing a hand across the back of his

neck, he admitted, "I've wanted to do that for weeks. I'm sorry I've taken advantage when you're still emotionally wrought."

Rebekkah shook her head. "I'm sorry. I think I needed that as much as you wanted to do it."

She could feel the heat enter her cheeks at her words. André smiled a gentle, understanding smile. "How about I save that for later and offer you this instead?"

He opened his arms.

She gladly went into them.

He engulfed her, holding her tightly. She didn't care about the mild pain it caused her injured body. Her body might protest, but her ravaged emotions bathed in the security.

After what seemed like forever but was surely only a few minutes, André released her. Rebekkah tottered to the nearest sofa and collapsed.

André hurried into the closest bathroom and returned with wet towelettes for her knees and hands.

"Did the man rob you?" André pulled out his cell phone.

Rebekkah reached out, laying her fingers over his hand to stop him from dialing. Seeing the tinge of blood she left, she quickly pulled back and cradled the injured hand awkwardly. "I fought, trying to claw my way out from under him. I guess I scraped my hand."

André said something under his breath before dropping next to her and pulling her into his arms. With one of the towelettes he dabbed at her injured hand.

She didn't protest.

Tentatively he asked, "Was he trying to—to…"

Realizing where this was going, she shook her head. "No. André he was here to warn me off the case I'm—we're working on."

"What?" Setting her where he could study her face, he waited for an explanation.

"He told me to stop researching the case. Said *he'd* cover it up again if I found anything." She cleaned her knees gently, silently bemoaning the loss of the expensive panty hose. She used fresh towelettes to wipe the grit, grime and blood from her hands.

"Again? Who?"

Rebekkah shook her head. "I was going to tell you what I found tonight, but after this…" Meeting André's eyes, she said softly, "I received a letter from a person in Alaska informing me that a man who once worked for Kittering had information that proved Kittering and their parent company knew what was going on. He talked with someone here and sent the information with the guarantee that this company, Watson and Watson, would back off and allow them to pay for damages. Someone covered it up."

"Why send them to us and not the other side?"

"The person who sent me the letter said he knew someone here and trusted them. That's all they knew."

"My father wouldn't cover up something like that," André argued, though he didn't sound so sure.

"The other partners were here, as well, at that time. Who knows? It's simply information that we have to follow up."

"How? We don't have anything on the informant."

"Yes. We do. We have his name."

André paused, his eyebrows going up. "You have his name?"

Rebekkah nodded. "Jacob Farley. He lives out in the wilderness, having quit back when all of this happened. He turned to hunting and trapping."

"Did you try to call him?"

Rebekkah sighed. "He doesn't have a phone."

Glancing at her still oozing knees, he said, "We can discuss this later. I'm going to call Dad and then the police."

"I'm going to clean up." She stood. She felt stiff, sore and still a bit wobbly. She kicked off her shoes and went into the rest room.

She slipped off her ruined hose, washed up then straightened her hair. Dark splotches on her gray suit made her look worse off than she was. Slipping the jacket off, she thought she looked somewhat better.

She wondered if the jacket and skirt would come clean and if she'd ever be able to wear the suit again.

Taking a deep breath, she returned to the waiting area.

André was just closing his phone as she entered.

"What did your dad say?

"He's appalled at what happened, Rebekkah. He cares for you a lot."

He sounded surprised. Rebekkah couldn't help but smile at André's discovery. "And I think a lot about him."

"He doesn't want us working at the offices. He said if you were attacked once, you could easily be vulnerable here."

"I'm not going to stop working just because some jerk threatened me."

"No. Not at all." André crossed to her, took her by the elbow and escorted her to the sofa. Sitting in a chair next to her, he leaned forward and said, "My dad actually wants us to get to the bottom of this. He swears he didn't cover up anything, that it had to be all lies. But he wants us to go to Alaska and find out."

"Alaska?" Stunned, Rebekkah simply stared.

André nodded. "He's calling Michael now to have him see to the arrangements. It looks like tomorrow, if you're up to it, we'll be taking the private jet on a long trip."

Alaska, with André. Just her and André. Sitting here hurting from head to toe she couldn't help but think how heavenly that sounded—her and the man she'd just kissed, the man she was attracted to, alone for several hours on a plane.

With a smile she said, "I can't wait."

Chapter Eleven

Rebekkah certainly could have waited. She could have waited a lifetime for today. More than a lifetime. It seemed things weren't going to go their way at all on this case.

Not at all.

"Someone's out to kill us!" she cried over the misfiring engine.

They had almost made it. Almost. Over Alaska, another thirty miles to the small landing strip where a guide awaited them to take them to Jacob…and now this.

"I think you may be right," André said, working to keep the plane in the air. "Hold on. I'm going to radio for help."

The engine went silent.

"Uh-oh."

"Understatement," André muttered, snatching the mike. "Mayday, Mayday. This is… Oh, no!"

The trees loomed up at them. André dropped the mike and pulled on the controls. "Watch for a clearing." Grabbing the mike again, he quickly finished the plea for help as they skimmed the tops of the trees.

He worked hard to keep the plane up as his eyes skimmed for an area to land. But there was nothing except more trees.

There was nowhere to land.

Nowhere they could make it safely to ground.

The tense expression as André gritted his teeth told the entire story. There was no hope, but he was going to try.

"Oh, God," Rebekkah prayed, her voice catching as she heard the scrape of the first tree on the base of the craft.

"Hold on!" André shouted.

"Help us!" Rebekkah cried.

The sound of metal creaking and what felt

like turbulence were the only warnings that they had hit the trees. Then everything happened at once.

Rebekkah careened against the wall, smashing her head. The tiny seat belt barely managed to hold her in place. Colors—green, brown, white—all mixed together in a dizzying display and swirled around them.

Pain exploded in her face as something hit her and then there were sounds of metal grinding, twisting and popping.

A large bump tossed her in the air, and the only thing keeping her from hitting the ceiling was her trusty belt. And then they were spinning again before they abruptly stopped.

Rebekkah felt skin give way as her head met with metal, and then there was blackness.

André couldn't believe he was still alive. At least, he thought he was alive. His face was bleeding, and one leg was pretty banged up. Managing to get his seat belt off, he glanced at Rebekkah, who had a head injury.

Every bone in his body ached. He felt like the seat belt had permanently imprinted itself on him, and his stomach felt as if it had been pushed up in his throat.

Taking a deep breath, he worked to keep from throwing up—or passing out.

He reached across to Rebekkah and tugged her belt off. Her caramel-colored skin was tinged with debris and blood. Brushing at stray pieces of wood and pine needles, he gently smoothed her dark hair. "Rebekkah?" he whispered, and his voice hurt. Had he shouted as they hit the ground?

Reaching up he realized his neck was tender. Debris, most likely.

"Bekka, sweetheart?" he whispered and then as gently as possible he pulled her into his arms. Turning, he stepped through the hole in the back, over the large branch that protruded all the way from the front to the ground directly behind his seat. The limb had come in at an angle, some of the branches hitting Rebekkah, but the bulk passing between them. It had smashed most of the front of the plane. Nothing was left of the back. The plane ended directly behind them.

Wobbling, he carried Rebekkah from the plane—or what was left of it.

About the only thing left were the two seats they had been sitting in. Everything else was in the trees and along the ground. He could see the twisted, unidentifiable pieces of luggage and metal and smell the strong smell of jet fuel.

"Thank You, God," André whispered, feeling that this was a miracle. "Thank You," he whispered. They hadn't caught on fire. How, he didn't know. None of the broken branches or tree trunks had ended their life, and somehow they'd ended up on the ground. Yes, it was a miracle.

Turning to his passenger he examined her, running his hands over her legs and hips, her ribs and arms, finding nothing except the head injury. Just as he finished examining her, she moaned.

"Rebekkah, honey?" He slipped his hands to her head, cupped it, then gently rubbed it.

Rebekkah blinked and shuddered. "We're alive."

"It's a miracle," André whispered, still trembling and doing his best not to show it. Rebekkah needed his support, not his fear.

Struggling to sit up, she glanced at the plane. And then did the same thing André had done. She started praising God. André pulled her into his arms and joined her, feeling very, very thankful at the moment. He'd almost lost his life and the woman he held.

The woman he cared very much for.

The woman he loved.

What a terrifying realization. He'd lost his first love because of doubts and fears, but the woman he loved with all of his heart, all of his soul, all of his body...he'd almost had her snatched away from him because... "Someone tampered with the plane."

"What?" Rebekkah pushed away, staring at him as if he'd lost his mind. André winced and turned, dropping to the ground next to her. "You don't know that for certain. Surely—"

"Surely we can't have so many coincidences happen to two people. Your car, then you are mugged and now this?'' André's back hurt, he realized, and his shoulders, as well. As a matter of fact, his neck was killing him.

Rebekkah swallowed. ''I think I'm going to be ill.''

André didn't feel very far behind her on that one as his stomach, which had been in his throat, now told him it was where it should be, twisting and cramping as it did. ''Take deep breaths,'' he muttered, trying to follow his own advice. ''It's your body's reaction to everything that's happened.''

Rebekkah once again thanked God for saving them. André couldn't blame her. Seeing all that was left of what had once been a plane chilled him to the core.

André continued to sit in silence and simply breathe until the worst of the nausea passed.

''What now?'' Rebekkah's voice sounded small and scared, but when he looked at her, her eyes were clear and sharp as she glanced around the man-made clearing.

"Well, we got a Mayday off, I'd suggest staying here until someone finds us." She was strong, he'd give her that. He didn't think he knew a single woman who would be able to think about anything after what had just happened. Any woman except this one.

"Do you think that'll happen? Will someone find us?"

"I hope so," André said quietly. He set a hand on her thigh and gave it a squeeze. "It'll just take time."

Rebekkah rubbed at her head, saw the blood and winced.

"You're bleeding, sweetheart. Stay still. I'll be right back."

"But..."

"Don't argue." André pushed himself to his feet. The first few steps were hard. His body was stiff and sore. But after a few yards he stopped trembling. He traced the line of debris until he found some pieces of cloth. He gathered them, returned to her side and dropped down next to her with a sigh of relief. His knees were bothering him.

"Here, try holding this on the spot on your head."

"How bad is it?"

"A goose egg," he affirmed. "You're a regular black and blue after yesterday and now this."

She didn't laugh as much as he tried to get her to. Instead, she frowned. "It's going to get cold out here," she muttered.

"It's already cold out here." Thankful he had his jacket on, he looked to see how torn up it was. "Oh, to be back in hundred-degree weather in Texas."

"I wouldn't go that far," Rebekkah argued, the first small smile curving her mouth.

André thought how inane their conversation was. Probably because both of them were still coping with the fact that they'd almost lost their lives.

"We need to collect what we can from the wreckage so we don't freeze to death tonight. Do you feel up to helping me?"

Rebekkah nodded. "It beats sitting here."

André was still dealing with all his emotions as he limped to where Rebekkah sat. He loved this woman. Someone had tried to kill them. They were stuck in a cold, empty wilderness.

Too many things bombarding his mind at once.

"You're limping."

Glancing at Rebekkah, he followed her gaze to his knee. Concentrate on one thing at a time, he thought. He'd get through it if he stuck to immediate problems. They both would. "I banged it up pretty bad. It's not broken, just bruised."

"Your own goose egg," Rebekkah said, worriedly, "only on your leg."

Studying the large swelling, André acknowledged that what Rebekkah said was true. "But we're alive."

"Yes," Rebekkah agreed. "We're alive."

"Well, let's go," André said and helped her up. Together they followed the line of destruction, finding clothes, metal, supplies, whatever had survived the crash.

And with each yard they explored, André's foreboding grew. This wasn't an accident. Someone had tampered with their plane. The only person it could have been was the person who'd sent them on this trip in the first place.

He didn't want to believe what his mind was telling him as they gathered supplies to wait for the search party.

But it was the only thing that made sense.

He wanted to rail against it, deny it, but... how could he?

"What are you thinking?" Rebekkah asked as they brought their fourth load of miscellaneous articles to the point of impact.

"The crash," André admitted, though he wasn't sure he wanted to tell her everything he was thinking.

"You're wondering who did it?"

Grimly, André nodded.

Rebekkah dropped the clothes she had found and moved to André. Taking his hand in hers, she said, "You can't prove it wasn't an accident. Please, André let's have faith that it was accidental until it's proven otherwise."

"There's not enough left to prove anything," André muttered darkly.

Squeezing his hand, she replied, "Trust God to see us through this."

"I trust God, Rebekkah. I'm just afraid of what we're going to find out when we get back."

"Please, André. Don't consider your father in this. It still could all work out and prove he's innocent of everything."

Evidently what he'd thought had gone through her mind, as well. "We call my dad last night telling him it looks like indeed our company covered up something. He suggests we come here and then this?"

"We can't prove anything. Why would he send us here unless…"

"Exactly," André said when she hesitated. "Unless it was to bury the evidence."

"Unless it was what he said all along. He wants the truth out. André, your dad has started going back to church. His entire life has changed. Please don't accuse him of this and make the rift between you two wider."

André pulled back, wincing slightly. "I don't know. Is my dad capable of this?" Running a hand through his hair, he admitted how much that thought ate at him. It emptied him out, leaving a hollowed shell where his heart had been. He didn't want to believe it but...

"You know what I thought of as we came down, André?" Rebekkah asked, laying a hand against his back.

He was desperate. He wanted to hear a good explanation that would make his father look innocent. It was too incredible to believe that his father would hurt him.

"What, Bekka?"

"I thought about my mom. How it was growing up in the inner city. About all of the men she had there and how angry that had made me. I wanted to hate her for the embarrassment she caused me, André. I wanted to get as far away from her and that life as possible. Climbing the social ladder as a lawyer was the best way. I didn't want anything to do with any of that. I didn't want it touching me or soiling me so I didn't even visit my mom anymore."

"Rebekkah," André started as he turned toward her.

"As the plane was crashing, all I could think of was that I wanted my mama. I wanted to be in her arms, telling her how sorry I was. I wanted to apologize for not trying to help her out of the situation she was in, but running from it instead. I wanted to tell her I loved her one last time."

"You'll get that chance, Bekka," André said and hugged her.

"That's only part of my point. André, God gave us a second chance. Please, don't continue to look at your dad through the dark tinted glasses but take this chance God gave you to believe your dad and start over."

André nodded, liking what she said. "Yes. Yes, you're right. There has to be another explanation."

"That's right. Believe that. Determine in your heart, André, that we're going to get back to your dad and my mom. We're going to confront them about the past. I'm going to make it up to my mom, the way I've been, and you're going to sit down with your father and discuss the pain and betrayal you feel."

André held her close, squeezing his eyes shut, thinking how much sense her words made out here in the wilderness, just the two of them in the low temperatures of summer. "What did I do before you came into my life, Bekka?" André murmured into her dark head of hair.

"Same thing I did before I met you, André. We both survived by making law our life."

Realizing he was noticing more than her hair, like the shape of her body and how soft it was against his, he quickly stepped back.

"Why don't you separate all our supplies while I gather wood for a fire?"

Rebekkah studied him. "Very well. But promise me, André. Give your dad the benefit of the doubt until we talk to him."

André smiled. "How could I refuse?" Turning, he thought Rebekkah could convince him of almost anything.

When had he allowed that woman under his skin?

How was he going to admit to her that he loved her?

Would they even make it out of here alive?

First things first. Gather wood.

Going into the woods, he reminded himself, one thing at a time. But it didn't look as if life was going to allow that.

Chapter Twelve

The crackling of the fire filled the small clearing with its noise, allowing Rebekkah to relax into André's arms.

"Are you warm enough?"

Rebekkah smiled. "Warm enough."

"Did the aspirin help?"

Rebekkah nodded against André's chest. "My head feels much better. How about you?"

"The knee is barely throbbing."

"Funny that it's late evening and still so bright out," Rebekkah murmured, staring at the sky.

They'd been here for nearly eight hours. In the time they'd waited, hoping for someone to find them, they'd come to an unspoken agreement to see to the basics.

They'd found nearby bushes that had berries but weren't sure if they were edible. Deciding, on the optimistic side, that they would be gone before they had to find out, they worked instead at staying warm.

Rebekkah found she enjoyed being in André's arms. After they found her purse and the aspirin, they both felt somewhat better, though still a bit shell-shocked over all that had happened.

André's hand continued to move up and down her arm, bringing warmth. "You know," he said, "I've had more happen to me in the last month of being with you than I have my entire life."

Rebekkah smiled into his chest, setting her arms more firmly around him within the confines of the blankets they'd found in the back part of the plane. They smelled a bit like jet fuel and pine, but they were serviceable. "I have to admit to the same thing."

André's deep, rich chuckle rose, rumbling against her ear. "My life has been different. Sitting here looking around, I have to wonder when was the last time I took time off from work. Most likely when I found out about…Sarah."

"You care a lot for her," Rebekkah replied quietly.

"She's a good friend. I can't stop thinking, though, that if I had died in the crash, I'd have nothing to show for my life."

Rebekkah gave him a small squeeze. "Don't say that."

"It's true. As you said earlier, my life with my family is in shambles, and we're not even sure if…"

If his father was the one who had nearly killed him, Rebekkah finished silently. "I know, André."

Sobering, he said, "We have to get back to civilization and make contact with my father. I have to find out the truth."

"The only way to do that is to find out the truth about this case."

The smoky smell of the fire filled the air

as André contemplated quietly. The occasional chilly wind swept over them. And if Rebekkah wasn't mistaken, it looked as if it had gotten a bit darker.

"You're right."

"Hm?"

"About the case."

Rebekkah leaned back and glanced at André. "What about it?"

New determination sparkled in André's eyes. "The case is what this is all about. We have to find out what's going on. I think we need to drop out of sight until we can figure out everything."

"Drop out of sight?" Alarmed, Rebekkah wiggled away and sat up, immediately regretting it as the chilly air surrounded her body.

She didn't attempt to reposition herself in his warmth, though. "What do you mean? We can't just drop out of sight."

André shifted slightly. "We need time to heal. We need time to find information. Whoever is trying to end this investigation has tried twice now to hurt you and nearly killed us this last time. I think we should investigate this on our own until we find out the truth, then contact my dad.''

''But…but…but that's ridiculous, André! He'll be worried and want to know if you're alive or dead.''

André sighed. ''How about if we get a message to my parents and your mom that we're okay, but just don't tell them where we're at? Then we can buy some time to find out what's going on.''

Rebekkah hesitated.

''Look, your head injury isn't going to let you do anything strenuous for awhile. I saw how weak you were when we were trekking to gather things. If my knee hadn't been so bummed up and I hadn't been worried about leaving you alone I wouldn't have let you come at all.''

Rebekkah gasped in outrage. When her head started pounding she wished she hadn't.

''See?'' André said smugly.

''I'm watching you limp, too, André,'' Rebekkah chided, ''and see? Your knee is twice as swollen as it was earlier.''

"My point exactly. We can find somewhere to recuperate and investigate from there."

Although Rebekkah would love to forget this case and never see it again, she was afraid to stop investigating. Who knew if they had too much information? Would whoever had caused the crash keep trying to hurt them? "I guess there's no way around it, is there?"

André reached out and nudged Rebekkah, attempting to get her back in his arms. She resisted for a moment then gave in. "No, sweetheart, there is no other way."

"If someone finds us—" Rebekkah said.

"*When* someone finds us," André corrected.

Rebekkah started to respond when she felt André's lips on her forehead. Desire stirred in her. She admitted to herself that his simple touch ignited fires in her. Attraction.

It was something God had put in them. But it could get in the way at times. Especially times like this when giving in would be so easy.

"Oh, André," she finally whispered on a sigh.

"I know, sweetheart," he replied just as quietly. "I didn't expect it to happen, either."

Running his hands down her back, he continued, "But sometimes, when God puts someone in your path, He has plans that don't coincide with your own."

"I'm just not ready," she admitted.

"I didn't think I was either...until now."

Rebekkah stiffened. Surely he wasn't intimating what she thought. She was attracted to him, but more than that, she wasn't ready. He couldn't be, either.

"I—" She wasn't sure what she was going to say. And it would stay that way, because at that moment the sound of underbrush rattling caught their attention.

"What?" Rebekkah asked, carefully twisting toward the sound.

"I don't know. An animal, maybe?" André said, and nudged Rebekkah away. He looked around for a stick and found one just as a huge bear of a man broke into the clearing.

"So there you are!"

Stunned at the sudden appearance of the man, Rebekkah gaped. He was easily six foot six inches and nearly as wide as a bear. He had a bushy brown beard and bright red nose and was dressed in thick woolen clothes and dark scuffed boots. Two big woolly dogs came trotting up behind him, tongues lolling as they grinned at them.

"Yes. Here we are. Were you looking for us?" André asked curiously, stick still in hand.

The man, instead of being threatened, let out a loud guffaw. "Me and about half the population around here. I'm glad it was me who found you."

"Ah, well. We're simply glad we were found. I'm André and this is Rebekkah," André offered, still holding the stick.

The man stepped forward and stuck out his hand toward Rebekkah. "And I'm Jacob Farley, the man you've come to see."

"Jacob—" Rebekkah started.

"Farley," Jacob finished.

"The witness?" André asked.

"Exactly!" Jacob replied.

With great relief, Rebekkah sagged against André. "We've been rescued, André, by the person we came to see."

"That's great," André said and dropped the stick, hugging Rebekkah.

Along with the sound of crackling fire, the sound of Jacob's loud laugh filled the clearing, flooding Rebekkah with a sense of joy and peace that everything was going to finally start falling together.

If they could just stay alive long enough to find out the truth.

Chapter Thirteen

It seemed to take forever to walk the first half-mile of the three miles to Jacob's house. Three miles. Rebekkah still couldn't believe he was that close to their crash sight.

"So, you think that there plane of yours was tampered with?" Jacob asked André as the three of them walked.

Rebekkah found herself glad the dogs stayed so close to assist her in walking. They seemed to sense her need of help as they trekked up and down the craggy landscape.

"It looks like that's a possibility," André confirmed. His leg had been bandaged up, and Jacob had fashioned a walking stick to help him steady himself.

"Just a quarter mile more and we'll be to the truck, and then we can drive the rest of the three miles," Jacob encouraged. "I couldn't go off road in this area. It's a shame you couldn't have made it a half-mile more in the plane. There was a spot where you could have attempted a better landing. It's a pure miracle you didn't die in that crash as is."

"I certainly concur," André said. He froze, wincing, when he stepped wrong. He took a deep breath and let it out slowly. Rebekkah paused, leaning against one of the dogs, nibbling her lower lip in worry as she watched. But André was okay. After a second breath he gave her an encouraging smile and started up the path again.

Jacob was a tender man. Rebekkah watched the concern on his face and the way he helped André over some of the worst of the fallen trees. She felt safe with him.

It hadn't dawned on her until after they'd started their trek that this man could have been a threat. André had suspected it immediately, she realized. Otherwise he wouldn't have held onto the stick so long.

Her head was throbbing again, but her blood was pumping from the workout she was getting. At least she could say she was warm.

"You know, if I had thought someone would react the way they did, I sure wouldn't have agreed to see you if you flew up here. That's why I quit Kittering so many years ago and moved out here. Things were going bad. Someone suspected I didn't agree with what was going on. I decided it was best if I just dropped plain outta sight."

"Why didn't you testify?" Rebekkah asked. "If you knew something why wait this long?"

The huge man sighed. Those once sparking blue eyes changed to a deeper hue of regret. "My wife was ill. When I found out she was, I just wanted away from everything. I wanted to spend what time I had left with her. We came out here where no one could find us. In the boondocks, so to speak."

"I'm sorry," Rebekkah murmured, hearing the grief in his voice.

"I'm not. Well, not exactly. She and I had the best time of our twenty-year marriage while she was sick. We had hoped getting away from everything...well, that she'd get better, but she went on to a better place, and that's something I have to accept."

"That's a gift there," Rebekkah said, noting André was huffing as he came through the last bit of trees and to the dirt road.

Rebekkah saw the truck and headed for it, never so relieved to see such a beat-up rusted-out relic in her life. The two huge dogs raced ahead, dancing around the truck as they waited on their master.

Jacob whistled, and both dove into the back of the truck. Rebekkah walked to the truck and leaned against it, waiting for Jacob to unlock it. She couldn't describe the relief of finally being here, away from the crash site. Alaska was beautiful country, she thought, but right now all she wanted was to get in somewhere and sit down. She ached from head to toe.

Jacob came around to her side and opened the door.

Surprised, she realized it was unlocked. Blushing, she climbed in, thinking that no one would rob them out here, so he probably never locked the door. André scooted in after her. Rebekkah liked the warmth of his body next to hers. As she adjusted herself in the middle of the cab, she didn't mind when he slipped an arm around her shoulders. She found herself leaning slightly into him as Jacob folded his huge body into the cab next to her.

"How's the leg?" Rebekkah asked worriedly, glancing down to where André's other hand gripped his leg.

"Probably about as good as your head," he murmured.

His teeth were clenched and his face white. Rebekkah nibbled her lip but thought that only increased the pain in her head. Rubbing at her temples, she said, "Jacob, can you tell us what proof you have that shows our firm was negligent? That shows Kittering really was dumping pollutants?"

"I sure can," Jacob said as the engine roared to life. "I'll take you right out to one of their dump sites. But we'd better wait until tomorrow. It's near the middle of the night, and we all could use some sleep. And I think the local law would like to know you've been found."

Jacob reached for the citizen-band radio in his car. André stretched his arm past Rebekkah. "Wait," he said, tapping Jacob's hand, which had unseated the mike.

Jacob's bushy eyebrows shot up, his gaze going to André in question.

"I—we have a favor to ask."

Rebekkah shook her head. "Now isn't the time, André. We should wait."

"But we can't wait! It has to be now. Jacob," André said, turning his attention to the big man, "I'm not sure how safe it is for us after what's happened…"

"I sure can agree with you on that one, André, bud," Jacob drawled.

"Can you tell the person in charge of the search team that we're banged up and want a few days just to rest before we talk to anyone? Then can you tell us where we can find somewhere out of the way that's safe, somewhere we can stay until we recoup?''

Slowly Jacob nodded. ''That's not a bad idea. Tell you what. I have two other cabins on my land. Why not let me tell them I've put you up in one of those. I'll tell them you're okay but want some time to rest. While they're waiting on you I can show you everything you want to see. When you're ready I'll take you into town.''

''Yeah, that'd work. Tell them we've taken you up on a mini vacation and then you don't have to give away our exact location.''

Jacob grinned. ''I sure can. Don't you worry. Let me handle the rest.''

''Thank you.''

''Will that be putting you in any danger?'' Rebekkah asked.

''No, ma'am. I know everyone out in these parts. While I trust them all, I can see why you wouldn't. Of course, you'd have to go in the city eventually, and I can't guarantee you on those that live there. I think you're making a good choice.''

Rebekkah leaned against the seat. "Thanks."

Jacob gunned the truck as he grabbed the mike. In minutes he had explained everything. And in just as short a time they had arrived at one of Jacob's shacks—the one he must have called home, from the looks of it.

Shack was the only word Rebekkah could use to describe it. Made of logs, it looked to be about two rooms big. Smoke poured out of a chimney. On the east side a small barn and a garden looked odd in such a rustic place. At least to her, it did. He had a garden in Alaska. She would never have dreamed such a thing. And what was so amazing was that she was certain the plant that was big enough to fill her entire sink back home was a head of cabbage.

Jacob must have seen the odd look on her face because he commented, "I like having a garden in the summer. Besides, because of the long hours of sunlight everything grows really big." He chuckled and climbed out of the truck.

"Big is an understatement," Rebekkah murmured to André.

"A simple life," André murmured. "I can see why he and his wife had such a happy time."

"No neighbors, no noise. Little work to keep up the house, I'd bet. A garden and your basic chores."

Jacob pulled open the door to the truck and reached in to help André out. His leg had stiffened as he'd rode in the truck. Rebekkah watched him wince as he stretched out his leg. Carefully he put weight on it, limping the first few steps before gaining his balance. Slowly he made his way to the house. Rebekkah followed.

Rough, pastoral, the inside had a braided rug, a sofa, four chairs, a table and a cook stove. To one side a door led to a bedroom and a bathroom. That was it. Rebekkah gratefully sank into one of the overstuffed chairs, dropping like a rag doll, her body molding into the softness.

"I'm sorry I don't have more here. I'll make a nice pallet. You can have the couch, André and I'll let Rebekkah here have the bed."

"I can't take your bed," Rebekkah protested.

"Sure you can," Jacob argued.

"You can't fit on the sofa," Rebekkah said. "You'd be too uncomfortable. I don't mind the sofa at all."

Jacob looked unsure.

"Believe me," Rebekkah argued.

André who had just gotten his leg positioned, smiled wearily. "Believe her. Once she makes up her mind she's nearly impossible to convince otherwise."

Jacob gave in. "Then it's settled. Let me get some ice for that knee, and then we'll get you situated for the night. If you want a shower, it's right in there." He pointed. "And then we'll talk tomorrow."

Rebekkah nodded.

Jacob crossed to the kitchen and grabbed a bag, which he quickly filled with ice, returning almost immediately.

Rebekkah decided to leave the two men and accept the shower. She also accepted the shirt Jacob gave her, and slipped into the bathroom. The hot water felt wonderful, eas-

ing many of the harsh bruises she'd ac-
quired. It seemed only yesterday she'd met
André. Yet a lifetime, as well. Her life had
been turned upside down. She had been
through more physical dangers than in the
entire time she'd lived in the inner city with
her mom.

She had thought being a lawyer would
keep her out of harm's way, keep her safe,
make her someone with position and pres-
tige. Instead, she found herself mugged,
threatened, her car burned and finally the
victim of an airplane casualty.

So much turmoil. So much inner strife.
However, as the hot water beat down on her
she allowed the worry and pain to wash
away. And she prayed. She doubted she'd
have time for personal devotions tonight, so
she spent the time in the shower thanking
God for His intervention in the crash, for she
truly believed it was because of Him they
had lived. She praised Him for the place
they had to stay tonight, thanked Him for
caring for them as He did and then told Him
about her developing feelings for André.

With each hour she was with André she felt closer to him, and somehow, after that crash, she didn't think she'd ever be able to forget him. Or to cut him out of her heart.

She left everything in God's hands and finished her shower, then slipped on the huge shirt Jacob had given her as a gown.

She came out of the bathroom and realized Jacob had made up the couch for her. Floral sheets, a thick patchwork quilt and a plush pillow called out invitingly to her.

Feeling her exhaustion, she headed toward the makeshift bed and pillow, then settled onto the couch. It was as comfortable as the chair had been, cushioning her body with its softness.

"Jacob's in bed already."

"Mmm," Rebekkah managed to say, thinking somehow this felt more comfortable than any bed she'd been in.

"I'm going to shower. I'll be quiet," André said as he set the ice aside and started toward the bathroom.

"André" Rebekkah whispered as he reached the bathroom door.

"Yes?" He paused.

She saw the stubble on his normally clean-shaven face, the bruise on his left cheek, the cuts and scratches on the left hand that rested on the doorway and thought he'd never looked better. "See you in the morning."

André offered her a gentle smile. "Yes. You will."

He went in to take a shower. As she listened to the water running, Rebekkah prayed a simple prayer with one straightforward request. She prayed that André would find out his father wasn't guilty of what had transpired.

And then, before the water was shut off, Rebekkah drifted to sleep, secure that all would be well tomorrow.

Chapter Fourteen

They were still alive.

He wasn't sure if he was relieved or angry.

He'd tampered with the plane. But it was supposed to go down before they got to Alaska.

They should have been able to land at an airport.

Of course, had they both been dead it would have solved the problem.

But he didn't want to kill them.

Rage caused the blood vessel in his right temple to throb.

He couldn't get it right.

Unbelievable.

A simple task.

Get them off the case.

Oh, he was interested in the case. However, he thought that André would get tired of it after a cursory glance and then go on.

Who would have guessed he and Rebekkah would devote so much time to it?

He saw the attraction and figured by now the two would be so involved nothing else would matter.

His mistake.

And now they were in Alaska.

He was going to have to hire someone to help him, someone to keep an eye on them while they were up there.

He could do that without anyone finding out. He had contacts.

He'd hire someone and make sure they kept an eagle eye on those two.

If anything happened, he wanted to be the first to know, the first to react....

"It's been three days. When do you think Jacob will be back?"

Setting aside the legal pad he'd been writing on, André glanced at Rebekkah, who stared out the window. "He said he had a few errands to do and then some runs to make and it shouldn't take more than a few days. I would imagine another day at the most."

"You said that yesterday," Rebekkah muttered.

André lifted an eyebrow in surprise, the corner of his mouth kicking up in a grin. "In a foul temper?"

Rebekkah turned, shooting him a glare. She crossed the room and flopped down on the sofa. "So you get to see the real me. Don't think to use it in court," she warned.

André smiled. "I find it endearing."

"Yeah," Rebekkah drawled, "like you'd find salt endearing in your glass of water. Give me a break."

André chuckled. "Jacob probably decided we needed the rest. We were both a bit worse for wear when he found us." He stretched, thinking his knee was almost completely normal again. The crash seemed like a distant memory, yet one that crept up at the oddest times—like when he was eating a meal and thinking how that meal could easily not have happened, or showering away the bumps and bruises.

Or when he looked at Rebekkah.

He had told himself to get through this case first and then admit his feelings when things were on an even keel. But being alone in the cabin with her for three days, watching her pace, clean, fidget and stand at that window for hours... Everything she did interested him. The way she tilted her head, clasped her hands behind her back and watched for someone to drive up the path to the cabin. The way she walked around the room, turning each knickknack this way and that, the way she had such a sharp eye for detail.

He'd been making notes on everything that had happened, hoping to keep his mind off the woman who sat, disgruntled, across from him. But it wasn't working. Her scent permeated the room, something floral that had obviously been left in the cabinet in the bathroom where she showered each morning. It was driving him crazy, the feminine scent, reminding him of how lonely and empty his life was without a life mate there with him.

It was too easy to imagine what it would be like, just Rebekkah and him, together like this, in their own house.

He pushed to his feet and crossed to the window to stare out, thinking that by turning his back he might be able to talk to Rebekkah without the urge to kiss her.

"It's almost dark out," he commented, staring at the twilight. "We both should already be in bed sound asleep."

Hearing his words, he winced.

"Don't worry. I know what you meant," Rebekkah murmured. She stood and walked across the room, grabbed an extra jacket and pulled open the door. "It's hard to sleep when it's still bright out, no matter how tired you are," she added before heading out to the front porch, right into his view.

With a resigned sigh he crossed to the coatrack and grabbed one of the coats. He went onto the porch and sat on the wooden bench. "I suppose you get used to all of the sunlight after awhile."

Rebekkah sighed and dropped next to him on the bench. He gave in to his desire and slipped an arm around her. She automatically leaned into him. "So how do they get used to all of the dark the other part of the year?" she asked. "At least twilight is finally here," she muttered.

"It must be hard, so much light and then dark..."

The sudden light in the sky caught André's attention. "What's tha—" He stood, stunned. "Wow," he finally murmured, moving to the edge of the porch.

Rebekkah rose and moved up next to his side and stared too. "The aurora? I've never seen it but read about it. That's got to be what we're seeing."

André nodded, gazing at the greens and blues that shifted and moved overhead in the darkening sky. He had never seen anything so beautiful, so dazzling.

"God's handiwork," Rebekkah murmured of the ions bouncing off the atmosphere.

"To say the least," André agreed.

André slipped an arm around Rebekkah and moved so he could pull her against him. He hugged her close. It seemed right, since the accident, that he touch her like this. He wasn't able to hide his feelings like before. He found he wanted to hold her, touch her, make his feelings known.

Rebekkah wasn't pushing him away physically or emotionally like she had before, either. Evidently since the crash some sort of fragile barrier had been broken that allowed more of their true feelings to shine through.

Like now.

Wrapping his arms around her, he rested his chin next to her cheek and whispered. "We came up here to work. Who would have thought we'd be treated to something so special?"

Rebekkah brought her glance around to answer but suddenly stiffened.

"What is it?" André asked, concerned.

"My foot. A cramp. Take me inside," she

said, and pulling herself free, she grabbed at his sleeve. She turned and limped toward the door.

"Slow down, Bekka, let me check it out," André protested.

Rebekkah didn't slow down, as she went into the house.

Exasperated, André went after her, only to have her pull him inside and slam the door, then bolt it behind him.

She reached over and pulled the drapes.

The hairs on André's neck stood up. "What is it?" he demanded quietly.

"I'm certain I saw someone out there, near the tree line. Something moved."

Agitated, Rebekkah crossed and checked the windows to make sure they were locked, then flipped out the lights before crossing to the sofa.

André carefully pulled the curtain back and studied where Rebekkah said she'd seen something. It was too dark to see anything now. If someone was out there, it had been amazing that Rebekkah had seen them.

Going to the sofa, André dropped down

next to her. "Rebekkah," he said softly, catching her hands, forcing her to turn her attention to him. "We're in the wilderness. Are you sure it wasn't a bear or something? I mean, maybe what you saw wasn't human."

He didn't want to doubt her, but then again...

"I—I don't know. It's just..." Rebekkah pulled her hands loose and smoothed the pants she wore. "When I saw something, whatever it was moved to hide. I guess it could have been an animal, but with all that's happened..."

André nodded and pulled her into his arms. "I don't blame you. I think I'd be a bit worried, too, if I saw something. As a matter of fact, I am a bit worried. Tell you what. Why don't we take shifts sleeping tonight? Would that make you feel better?"

"You really think I'm going to sleep after that? Do you think you'll really sleep?"

André chuckled. "If I sit here and hold you," he affirmed. "So, humor me. Let me hold you through the rest of the night."

She grinned, albeit a bit nervously. "If I hadn't seen it what would you have made up just to have your way with me?"

André gave her a wolfish glance. "I'm sure I could find a way."

Rebekkah smacked him on the chest.

"Ow," he murmured, making a hurt face.

She chuckled, more relaxed. "You're right. I'm going crazy. It was probably a deer or moose or something like that."

Relieved she had calmed down, André finally admitted, "You scared me when you took off inside. I guess we're both a bit jumpy." Not allowing her time to respond, he jumped into the next subject. "So, tell me something about the first guy you dated."

"Hey!" Rebekkah protested, pushing away.

André chuckled and pulled Rebekkah back into his arms. "Come on. You tell me, I tell you," he bargained cajolingly.

Rebekkah scowled. "I don't believe you."

"I won't lie to you, Bekka. Come on. Confess."

He could tell she was considering it the way she shifted her gaze away and slipped into a thoughtful mood.

"It was a disaster," she finally admitted.

"How so?" André asked, not having thought she'd admit to something like that.

"I had lied to the guy about where I lived. I didn't want him to know. So, I slipped several streets over where I waited for him to pick me up. I should have known lying would get me in trouble. He was a nice guy. He wanted to meet my parents, and I refused. That started the evening off on a bad foot. I worked hard to avoid some of the people I knew at the school dance, doing my own dance to keep my private life just that. But it was on the way home that disaster happened." Rebekkah sighed, and André tried to imagine the life he knew she'd come from. Ashamed about her mother and where she lived, wanting to break out of that lifestyle. There was a stigma in school—even in the school he'd attended. If your parents weren't what were considered normal for your environment, kids often didn't accept you.

"I wanted to be dropped off where he'd picked me up," Rebekkah continued, softer, "but he wouldn't leave me on the street. I got in an argument…just as one of the guys from my street drove up." Rebekkah shifted slightly, her body tensing.

"He delighted in causing trouble. He felt by playing the big bad guy on the block he'd get respect from the other kids. So, by putting me in my place by snubbing him and his group—his gang—he didn't mind at all telling my date all about my mom and where I actually lived."

André winced in sympathy. "I guess I can agree with you there."

"What's that?" Rebekkah asked.

André stroked her hair, enjoying the fact that she allowed him to hold her like this. "Your first date was a mitigated disaster."

"And your first date?"

"It went great," he said easily, and smiled at the disbelief in her stare. "I was cocky as a child."

"Oh, really?" she said with exaggeration.

"Hey, lay off the sarcasm." He couldn't

help but grin as he continued. "My parents didn't like the fact I wasn't dating, so I decided to go ahead and prove to them I could get whoever I wanted."

"And?" Rebekkah prodded when he paused remembering the day.

"I managed to get the daughter of a lawyer who was working on a case that just so happened to be in court against my father at the time. She and I went out, discussed cases and then…"

"Wait a minute. Discussed cases? How old were you? I thought this was about first dates." Rebekkah pulled back to look at him.

"It was a first date. I was sixteen. I was raised in the business, as was Lena."

"Lena?"

"Yeah. She hated her name, too. Anyway, she was in rebellion against her dad, who wanted to send her off to a boarding school, and I was in rebellion against my dad so he'd lay off the advice on my love life—or lack thereof."

"Love life at sixteen?"

He shrugged. "Dad kept suggesting I take this girl out who was the daughter of a friend of his. He likes to rule every area of my life. At any rate, we got to talking about cases our fathers had worked on, and the latest one came up. The family chauffeur had dropped us at the restaurant. Knowing my mom, I knew she'd be curious and question the chauffeur about the date.

"The chauffeur, of course, told my mom who the girl was. Not just her name but also her relation to the other lawyer. Philton was always a good guy, making sure to watch out for me for my dad. My mom, of course, told my dad. And both of our parents showed up at the same time."

"Oh, dear," Rebekkah murmured.

"They were incensed, certain each of us had put the other one's child up to subterfuge—especially when they found out what we'd been discussing."

"Your dad discussed his cases in front of you?"

"I hung out at the office a lot in those days and simply picked up stuff."

Rebekkah groaned.

"It's the closest I've ever come to my father laying hands on me in a physical way."

"You call that a success?"

André shrugged. "My dad didn't insist I date anymore—at least for awhile."

Rebekkah chuckled. "It sounds like we both had very interesting dating lives."

"Well, later I did. About the time I hit eighteen I discovered how much I enjoyed the women."

"That sounds so—so…"

"Male?" A self-satisfied grin on his face, he added, "Yeah. Well, that's a guy for you. But I wanted my career, so I never planned to settle down until I was to a certain point. That's when I found Sarah and decided she'd be perfect."

"Because of your dad and his interference?"

André thought about it. "Looking back, that might have been why I chose Sarah. We got along and were friends, and she definitely wasn't exactly what my dad would have picked. Yet she was what would look good on my arm as a lawyer."

His mood darkened. "I'm only glad she forgave me for that attitude and found real love. I can't imagine what our life would have been like had we ended up married."

"Sounds like God was watching out for both of you," Rebekkah said tenderly.

"Yeah." André frowned. "Wait a minute. We were only talking about first dates. I cry foul."

"Uh-uh," Rebekkah said and snuggled in his arms, releasing a loud yawn. "I didn't force that information out of you, you volunteered it. All's fair in and out of the courthouse."

André smiled, thinking Rebekkah might have won this round, but his ploy had worked. She was relaxed and ready to drift off to sleep—no longer worried about what she thought she'd seen outside. Now they could both get a good night's rest.

Chapter Fifteen

"So, are you ready to go examine the site?"

André who had just finished his shower and was dressed in fresh jeans and a shirt, nodded to Jacob. "More than ready. Glad you showed up this morning," he continued, crossing to a chair and sitting down to slip his socks on. "If you'd been gone one more day I'm afraid Bekka would have tried to trek there without you."

"I don't even know where it is," Rebekkah argued, drying the last plate and putting it up.

"I have to say the two of you look much better."

Rebekkah thought so, too. Jacob had shown up last night after she and André had fallen asleep. Five days had passed with no more sightings of anyone in the bushes. André had gone out and walked around the cabin the next day but could see no sign of anyone near the cabin.

"I need to call the sheriff real quick. I promised him you two would come in today and sign the statements you gave over the radio. Then after that we can leave."

Rebekkah had volunteered to do the dishes since she'd beaten everyone to the shower this morning. She was feeling great, like a new person. She admitted that the last five days were exactly what she'd needed. She hadn't realized she'd gotten so worn down by the stress until she'd had time to just sit and talk with André.

André.

What had happened in the last week between the two of them?

They were constantly touching, bumping

each other as they passed, André slipping his arm around her as if it were the most natural thing in the world.

And the worst part about it was that she accepted it. It felt so right and so good.

Except for the small part of her mind that warned her he still had unsolved issues with his father and she with her mother. Love didn't do well if you had a dirty plate to start it on.

Her attraction had developed to the point she was getting frustrated in more ways than one by his presence. She was glad that Jacob had shown up today as a buffer between them. She understood that God wanted people to care for each other. Unfortunately, along with that came all the desire two people could feel.

Last night as she'd been cleaning off the table she'd happened to glance up at André who'd been running soapy water, and caught his dark gaze filled with desire.

The shock of that gaze had ignited flames all the way down her body, and she'd known right then she was in trouble.

It was time to back off and get some breathing room or get into trouble with God.

She'd begged exhaustion and went to bed early.

André, she was sure, understood, because as soon as he was done with the dishes he'd gone out on the porch for a long while before waking her early this morning as he'd entered the cabin.

The strength of the attraction surprised her and had been a good wake-up call. She might try to ignore her feelings for him, but her physical response reminded her that she couldn't pretend there was nothing there between them.

"So how far is this site you want us to see?" André asked as he tied his sneaker.

"About two hours, actually. I moved far enough away so that it wouldn't affect my water."

"To the east of here?" André asked.

Jacob nodded. Finished with his call, he pushed his chair back and stood. "The sheriff said he'd meet us out here later this afternoon rather than our having to drive all the way into town after our little trek."

Rebekkah wandered to the front door and pulled it open, then stepped out on the porch and inhaled the deep pine smell that greeted her. The sounds of birds chirping brought a slight smile to her lips.

She was going to miss it up here.

She watched the tiny chipmunks scamper off and wondered if maybe they had those back in Texas.

Rebekkah couldn't remember the last time she'd taken time to enjoy life.

She'd been so worried about escaping her past that she'd forgotten to take time to enjoy the present.

Planning to rectify that as soon as she got home, she wondered how Drydan would take the announcement that she intended to take an extended vacation.

André arrived next to her, and together they walked to the beat-up truck. Piling in, they waited on Jacob, who was right behind them.

In minutes they were off and heading back the way they had come.

They eventually found a main road,

though Rebekkah saw no signs on it. However, it was the first paved road they'd been on, so she considered it a major highway. They didn't pass much on the way. The beautiful plains and rocky hills that slowly turned into mountains in the distance kept her attention. A lake and several small creeks also passed into view on their journey.

Eventually they turned off the main highway and followed a broken-down road that looked to have once been paved but now was more potholes than anything else.

Then they were turning into a forest onto what looked more like a nature trail than a road.

It got bumpy.

André's arm went around her.

Rebekkah braced her hands on the dash as they traveled over the uneven trail.

André's warmth felt good and right. She wanted to lean into it and stay there. Too bad it would end so shortly, she thought as Jacob suddenly slowed the truck.

The area they entered was in the middle

of a forest. Some grass covered the area, and a few small trees. It looked as if nature was attempting to reclaim an area that had once been claimed by man.

"Is this the area where the chemicals were dumped?" André asked.

When the truck had completely stopped, they all piled out. André pulled out a camera he'd borrowed from Jacob and started snapping pictures.

"Dumped isn't the exact word. The leftovers from the plant were stored up in drums and buried here. The problem was, those drums weren't the type that could guarantee no leakage."

"You're sure?"

Jacob sighed. The look that crossed his face suddenly made him look much more his age than the bright laughing man they'd originally met. Slowly Jacob rubbed a hand down his beard.

"It's a long story," he finally admitted. "The short version is we needed the money and I thought this a good job. All I had to do was sign a nondisclosure statement, which is common for almost any job. Then I'd be driving the truck once a week for Kittering. At the time I didn't question what was going on. It wasn't until nearly fifteen years later that people started getting sick."

"What was in the barrels? Did anyone ever manage to get samples?"

Jacob shook his head. "Nope. When there was noise of an investigation this place was cleaned up and the stuff dumped, most likely in the ocean somewhere."

"You have evidence of that?"

Again, he shook his head. "No, and this is actually private property we're on."

Rebekkah gaped. "We had better get off it, then."

"The plant owns the land from here on out. They don't use this area anymore. There used to be a small fence blocking the entrance at the road, but that went by the wayside. Since the plant has been majorly downscaled, few people even think about this empty land back here as being used or owned by Kittering."

André quickly scooped up some soil samples and then headed to the truck.

"I don't know that you'll find anything in that. Besides, what good will it do you now?"

André shrugged. "No good except for personal reasons."

Once they were all in the pickup, André continued his questioning. "You were the one who had the memos?"

Jacob nodded. "I asked a friend about them. He got them for me."

Jacob started the engine and headed toward Kittering. "Ed found some different things, but the one thing he showed me was a memo he found between Kittering and Langley about what was going on and the possible pending litigation."

Rebekkah pulled out a small tablet she'd had in her back pocket and started scribbling down all he said. "That's the memo that our company allegedly got?" she asked, cutting in on André's questioning.

She glanced up just in time to see Jacob point. "That's where I used to work. This plant employed most of the people around here at one time or another. A good place— or we all thought it was."

There were large buildings with tall pipes that had smoke coming out of some and flames out of different smokestacks. To her it looked like any one of the chemical plants or refineries that she'd grown up around.

"As for the memo," André prompted. "You sent it to us?"

"No. You see, Ed had a friend who said it'd be best to send it to your side."

"We were defending the company."

Jacob sighed. "As I said, we all thought the company was a good place. Only a few people were complaining. You know how it is, anytime there's a plant in the area you have some environmentalists who are going to complain and try to get it shut down. There's always some who don't like to have something like this in their backyard, even if it isn't currently causing problems. It ruins the environment."

Jacob scoffed. "These are the same people who curl up in their electric blankets and pull nice warm food out of the plastic containers they warmed up in their microwaves. Where do they think all of these luxuries come from?"

Sighing, he continued. "A lot of us just didn't believe the problems some of these people claimed. So, Ed's friend sent that memo on to someone at the company."

André was beginning to see. "An unintentional cover-up?"

"He knew someone there and said they'd know what to do with it."

"My dad wouldn't have taken the case if he'd thought Kittering was lying."

"I only know the memo was sent to your company."

"To who, exactly?" André asked.

Rebekkah waited to hear.

"You'll have to ask Ed."

André sighed. "What about his friend?"

"Died in a car accident shortly after the trial."

André leaned back in the seat, frustrated.

Rebekkah couldn't blame him. Two hours out here to take pictures of a plant and an empty field. A week of waiting to hear the story from Jacob, only to find out it wasn't Jacob who knew but a guy named Ed who knew the guy who sent the memo.

"At least we'll know who it was sent to after talking with Ed," Rebekkah soothed.

"Maybe," André replied grimly.

"Maybe," Rebekkah agreed.

Chapter Sixteen

❧

"Someone's been in the cabin."

"What?" André who had just pulled the film out of the camera, paused to look at Jacob.

"In here?" Rebekkah asked, dropping the pad and pen on the table and moving to where Jacob stood by the desk.

"My radio. It isn't on the band I left it on." Glancing around, Jacob tried to see if anything else had been touched.

Rebekkah was the one who spotted the problem. "Did you leave the desk drawer open? I'm sure it was closed until you got back last night."

Jacob glanced at it and shook his head. "Those are my financial statements. I only open it once a month to pay bills."

Rebekkah turned to André. He could read what was in her eyes. "Maybe I did see someone out there the other night," she whispered.

"See someone where?" Jacob asked.

"I thought I saw someone outside," Rebekkah told him.

"I convinced her it was just a deer or some other animal," André said. Angry with himself, he went to the door and scanned the area.

"Show me where," Jacob said quietly.

"I don't know. It might not be safe. We ought to just go on into town and get out of here now."

"Over there," Rebekkah said.

André scowled at her. When he saw the look on her face, he realized how worried she was.

Jacob went outside and crossed the clearing to where she'd pointed.

André followed, keeping Rebekkah close

to his side in case of any danger. Jacob carefully scoped out the area before confirming their worst fears. "There are definitely signs of human passage here. And in the last day or so." Lifting his gaze to André's he said, "I think we should get you in town to the sheriff. Looks like your time here has run out."

Rebekkah shivered.

André didn't argue. "We don't want you in danger. Let's go."

Jacob went inside and returned quickly. "The sheriff will be waiting. When we get there we can place a call to Ed and get you checked into a hotel."

As they got into the truck, Jacob said, "By the way, seems like your dad has contacted the sheriff several times in the last few days wanting an update on you."

"The sheriff doesn't know anything," André said as they started down the road, turning a different way when they came to the main highway.

"Your dad evidently didn't believe him. He's even contacted the local attorney about you. Seems they're old friends."

"From the case, I'm sure," Rebekkah added.

They sped along the highway, putting distance between themselves and the threat— or at least André hoped the threat was still back there somewhere and not following.

Rebekkah relaxed as they left the cabin behind. When André felt he could finally breathe easy again, he turned in the seat. Touching Rebekkah's chin, he pulled her attention to him. "I'm sorry I doubted you," he said softly.

Rebekkah dropped her gaze and shook her head. "No. I had convinced myself it was animals, too. I mean, after all that had happened…"

"After all that had happened," he continued when she didn't, "we had both hoped it was nothing, that we were wrong."

"André…" Rebekkah said softly, her voice cracking.

"I know how much my father means to you, but what else can it be? He talked to the sheriff. The sheriff is the only one who knew where we were besides Jacob."

"I'm sorry, André. It's just so hard to believe. We need to wait and talk to him first." Reaching out, she squeezed his leg just above his knee. "Do you think you can do that?"

Though André was hurting and still feeling a sense of disbelief, he needed to go ahead with a statement to her. Reaching out, he took her hand and lifted it to his lips. "If you're there with me, Bekka, I can do it."

Rebekkah's breath caught, and her eyes widened as he brushed his lips over her fingers.

"I don't think now..." She motioned with her head toward Jacob who was doing his best to ignore them.

"No, Bekka, now is the perfect time. I've tried not to say anything and give you room, but I have to admit my feelings for you have deepened. I love you, Bekka. If I'm going to get through this I am going to have to know where we stand."

"I—" Rebekkah's gaze turned from his to the windshield and then back. He saw a bit of a wild look as she started nibbling her lip. ''You know I have feelings,'' she finally said as if no one else were in the truck. ''But you have to settle this thing with your dad and me with my mom before we can go on.''

André opened his mouth to argue with her then realized that wasn't the type of confession he wanted from her. He was certain she felt more for him than she'd let on. He was sure she loved him, too. It was in the looks she gave him, the way she treated him, the yearning in her eyes when they were in the same room, the spiritual connection they'd seemed to develop as they'd started doing devotionals each night together while they'd been at the cabin.

But he couldn't force the words out of her.

God, please help me. My dad! I can't face that alone. I need her there with me. I need You with me. How can it be?

As he held her hand, André had an odd feeling he was missing something. What, he couldn't say. But something didn't feel right. Something wasn't falling into place. Perhaps it was the disquiet he felt in his spirit. He didn't know.

When Rebekkah slipped her arms around him and hugged him tight, he didn't reject the hug but pulled her tighter, praying that when they got into town everything would turn out okay.

In that moment he realized that whether his dad ever admitted he was right or wrong didn't matter. All André wanted right now was to hear his dad say he wasn't the one behind the danger.

Nothing else mattered.

He was afraid, though, if he talked with Ed first, he might find out he'd never be able to hear those words from his dad.

God help us, he prayed.

Chapter Seventeen

His source told him they'd been out to the site and then taken off for town.

This didn't bode well. They'd gone to the sheriff's office and then had checked into a hotel room. The sheriff had put a guard on the doors at the hotel. It seemed the sheriff wanted Jacob to stay in the room with André.

This didn't bode well, at all. They all knew something. That much was obvious.

The man cursed.

André was ruining it all.

Because of André everything would soon be out in the open.

Blast him for his pugnacious spirit.

He had to put an end to it. André had crossed the line. He had finally gone too far.

He just couldn't leave well enough alone.

At least if he stopped it now he might stop all of the truth coming out.

It was time for him to go to Alaska.

"Are you ready for the meeting?"

André stood in front of Rebekkah's door, cool, composed yet distant.

He'd been that way since she'd refused to say those three small words he'd wanted to hear. I love you.

That's all she'd had to say, and yet she'd choked at the last minute. Images of her mom telling so many men that had come back to her.

Images of that broken-down house they'd lived in.

She loved André. She did.

But then her mom had said she'd loved all those other guys that had come to her house—all those "uncles" she'd had. All she'd wanted to do was get away, make something of herself so she wouldn't end up like that.

But she realized it was more than that. Not only did she realize how she was running, but she was afraid to tell this man she loved him, not sure if she could say it.

She couldn't believe her mom's life still had so much power over her after all these years.

"Yes. Where are we supposed to meet?"

"A café two blocks away. Mac is going to be our escort."

One of the two police officers gave her a small salute. In his dark clothes he'd blend in well. He was average height with dark brown hair and skin. The other man's light blond hair and light skin reminded her of a German or Swede. He was also out of uniform, though she could tell he wore a gun under his jacket. There was a slight bulge there.

André on the other hand, in his nice-fitting jeans and sky-blue polo shirt, would probably stick out like a sore thumb. He had a black pullover that sported a nice red design but had it draped over his arm. Despite being in Alaska, he just couldn't get used to layering his clothes.

Rebekkah had pulled on a dark brown pullover to stay warm in the slightly chilled weather. She wore a long white button-down shirt and peach colored pants—along with some long underwear. She finally felt warm—the first time since they'd arrived.

She'd been so grateful to the detectives on duty yesterday evening as they'd offered to take them shopping for clothes. She and André had gone shopping right after he had called his father. Or tried to call him.

She paused to make sure her door was secure before turning to André. "Did you get through to your dad?"

André shook his head. "I finally got Mom's maid, though. She said Dad told her he had business and was out of town. Mom was in bed, the maid said, and couldn't come to the phone."

"I hope she's okay."

"I'm sure she is. Otherwise Stella would have told me."

Rebekkah frowned. "I wonder what's come up with your dad." It wasn't like Drydan to leave his wife. He doted on her, especially since he'd gotten his heart right with God.

"You know Dad," André said.

Rebekkah had prayed all night and was certain she did, indeed, know his dad. "Yes, I do. And I'm convinced your father doesn't know what is going on."

"You can't be that sure, Rebekkah," André argued as they headed down the ornately decorated hall, catching the elevator just as a couple got off.

"Yes, I can," Rebekkah answered. "I told Drydan to tell you this himself, but he refused. He asked Jesus into his heart, rededicated his life to God not too long ago."

Surprised, André stared. "Oh?" It was all he could manage to say.

Rebekkah could tell he was at a loss for words and felt peace at that. "Yeah. I was there. His entire life has changed. But you've been too busy to notice it, too filled with bitter memories of what he did to accept it's possible that he's turned over a new leaf.''

She saw André's anger ignite in his eyes. ''Just like you're too caught up in your mom's world to admit your feelings for me?''

She glared at him. ''At least I'll admit that.''

André opened his mouth and then closed it. ''I'm sorry. I said I wouldn't pressure you. You're right. That's none of my business. If my dad had really changed, though, he would have told me. I would see the change.''

Rebekkah wanted to yell at André. She knew, in her heart, his dad wasn't responsible. She could see André wanted to believe it, too, though so much of the evidence said otherwise. Staring at the plush red carpet in the elevator, she said, ''If you weren't so stubborn and would go around him more often, you would have already seen the change.''

The elevator door opened.

Exiting the elevator, Rebekkah noted the

two officers gave them room to continue their minor argument in private. And minor it was. Or so she kept telling herself. If she admitted it was a major argument she just might raise her voice. And she didn't want to do that in public. She always tried to stay calm and cool.

Only André had the ability to rattle her. And now he did it because of his stubbornness.

"Well, then, I guess I'll just have to spend time with him when we get back home to find out if he's really changed, won't I?" André said, interrupting her thoughts.

Rebekkah nodded, thinking she was finally getting somewhere with the thickheaded mule. "That would be a step in the right direction."

"And I'll leave you to spend time with your mom, then," he added.

Rebekkah's stomach fell at his words, the bluntness of them, the way they made her feel. "Yeah," she said, wondering if he meant that he didn't want to see her anymore.

Had that been what he'd meant? Had he meant she was to spend time with her mom because he didn't want to spend time with her anymore? He'd said he loved her and yet now was sending her off to Louisiana to spend time with her mom.

Well, she needed to see her mom and talk—but that's not what André had said.

His words had sounded final to her.

Off kilter from those words, she pushed through the door, swinging it wide, and stepped into the fresh air, where she didn't feel so confined.

"Wait a minute, Rebekkah," André said, and followed her.

"No." She was blunt but honest. She wasn't waiting. She was dealing with how hard those words had fallen on her heart. Had anyone else said something that sounded like that she never would have blinked an eye. She was used to all kinds of things from clients and other people.

But from André…

Love.

There was no doubt.

Her mom had never really cared from one man to the next. But if she lost André...

This was love.

André grabbed her by the arm and spun her around. "Yes. You'll wait. I didn't mean that."

"André I thought I taught you better."

Rebekkah and André both turned their heads toward the street, where Drydan had just stepped out of a cab. He paid the driver and then walked to where they stood. They were transfixed by the sight of Drydan in Alaska.

"Dad?"

Rebekkah was speechless.

What was Drydan doing here?

"Have you forgotten what I looked like in that short a time, son?" Drydan asked curtly.

André's back went up. "What are you doing here?"

Drydan scowled. "What do you think I'm doing here?"

André hesitated.

Rebekkah still didn't speak, watching the

emotions on Drydan's face as understanding dawned. "I was on the phone yesterday morning with the sheriff. And I had a long talk with your mom, as well. If you think I'm going to leave you here like this, when someone is obviously endangering you and Rebekkah, you're crazy."

André stood poised as if to act, then relaxed. "Tell me you aren't behind it, Dad," he asked. "Please. You've refused everything else. I'll never ask again if you just say it's not you."

Pain flashed in Drydan's eyes. His shoulders dropped. The man who usually looked so debonair and in charge of life suddenly looked old and tired.

"I can't believe you even have to ask me," Drydan said quietly.

"Dad." André's voice was tortured. "Just say you weren't the one who had Rebekkah's car torched or hired the mugger. Tell me you aren't the one who tampered with the plane or had someone watching us. Just say no, it wasn't me."

Drydan turned away from his son without

answering and walked off a couple of steps. Staring across the street, he refused to meet his son's gaze. The cool, crisp wind slapped Rebekkah's hair into her face, ruffled Drydan's coat as he stared at the brick buildings that lined the small Alaskan city street.

Rebekkah's stomach lurched.

Oh, no, God, please, she prayed silently. She slipped her hand around André's arm. She didn't want to believe Drydan had something to do with it. She couldn't believe that. He'd taken her under his wing, treated her like a daughter.

He wasn't capable of this.

He couldn't be capable of this.

She held onto André as much as she tried to give comfort.

André opened his mouth to say something. What, she didn't know, because everything happened so fast. Suddenly Drydan turned toward them and lunged at his son.

André stiffened, throwing his arms out, tossing Rebekkah away from him as if she was made of paper. Rebekkah flew through the air, hitting bystanders then landing hard on the cement sidewalk.

"Son!" The cry came out of Drydan's mouth at the same moment a shot sounded.

Screams erupted.

People fled, running, shouting. A nearby mother fell to the ground with her son, sobbing and trying to protect the child. Realizing what had happened, people looked around, alarmed, ducking out of the way of the panicked ones, trying to see who had been shot and if someone was still around with a gun.

Vaguely she saw one of the police officers who had been with them firing toward something or someone across the street. Then he took off, dodging cars. Rebekkah rolled to her knees and crawled over toward André.

Some people had started pushing the crowd back, calling out, "Make room."

The other police officer was talking into a mike on his shoulder.

She shoved past people's feet toward André.

As she got to him, she saw his face and shoulder were covered with blood.

For the first time she could remember, she

lost her composure in public. "André!" she cried and grabbed at him, scrabbling to get to him.

Drydan lay on top of him as if trying to protect his son.

Blood.

So much blood.

André moved.

"Please, André. Don't die. I love you. If you die I'll never forgive you."

"Get back in the hotel," the police officer said, and grabbed her arm as he shouted directions to someone standing nearby.

"No!" she shouted and jerked free. Grabbing André she cried out again. "André..."

"It's not me," André replied tersely.

"It's only a flesh wound," a woman said, who had dropped down next to Drydan and André and was leaning over them. Her serious gaze was directed toward the two men on the ground. Deftly she shoved her hair behind her ear and leaned closer to the two men.

"What?" Dazed, Rebekkah realized André only rubbed his head as he shoved with the other hand at his dad.

"I'm sorry, son. About Sarah. About everything. It wasn't me. I had no idea, though, that Michael was involved."

The woman, obviously someone the police knew, as they allowed her to help Drydan into a sitting position, examined the nick to Drydan's left cheek.

"Just sit still, Dad. Let this lady take care of you."

André sat up, and instead of taking his own advice he leaned forward and hugged his dad tightly. "How'd you know about Michael?" he asked.

"Michael?" Rebekkah said quietly, not sure anyone heard her. André was covered in blood but sitting up. She began to shake.

Drydan had blood on him, but he was talking, too.

"I didn't until I saw him just now. Your mom told me she's the one who got the memo last night." Drydan flinched as the woman probed his face then put a hankie the police officer gave her to his cheek.

Rebekkah realized a lot was going on around her. A patrol car had pulled up.

Across the street, André's stepbrother was being escorted from between two buildings.

A crowd had gathered and was being held back by volunteers who had been on the scene when everything had happened.

More police were wading into the crowd.

And André hadn't been shot.

But Drydan had been.

All the blood on André belonged to Drydan—not André.

The shaking in Rebekkah felt more like a palsy than mere tremors. Her stomach churned. The fear, the shock, the need to react to what happened built in Rebekkah.

Without warning, Rebekkah burst into tears. They weren't the gentle and simple tears a lady would cry. These were loud, like wailing sobs, something she had never dreamed would come out of her mouth. She had never in her life lost it like this. Not even in court.

Yet here she was like a blathering idiot, crying her eyes out, while Drydan and André looked on in shock.

"You'd better take care of her," Drydan

murmured, smiling then wincing. "We'll talk about this later."

An ambulance pulled up.

"That's going to need stitches. By the way, my name is Dr. Schwartz. I'll ride with you if you'd like," the young woman said.

"I don't need to go in that," Drydan argued.

"Go," André ordered, then moved to Rebekkah and pulled her into his arms.

Rebekkah didn't argue but collapsed gratefully against the hard, reassuring chest. Her hands climbed up and slipped around his neck, the neck that was slick with blood.

"Oh, no," she gasped through her tears. "No…"

That had been so close. She could smell the coppery smell, feel the blood on her hands. It made her grip him tighter.

"Looks like I'm going," Drydan said. "I just convinced him I'm not trying to ruin his life, so I suppose it wouldn't hurt to humor him."

Rebekkah heard the doctor laugh as she helped Drydan into the vehicle.

Still she cried. "You should go with him," she sobbed. "I told you he was innocent."

André hugged her tight. "And he almost paid with his life."

"*You* almost paid with your life, too," she yelled.

André hugged her tighter. "I'm okay, sweetheart. I promise you."

"You are not. You're covered in blood!"

"Dad's blood." André's grip tightened at his words.

She gasped as he nearly cut off her air supply. He immediately eased his hold on her. "I'm sorry. I'm being totally impossible." Taking a deep breath, she worked to get her sobs under control. She felt André shift and pick her up. He quickly crossed to a patrol car at the curb and with deft movements he maneuvered them into the back seat.

She adjusted herself, unwilling to let go of him.

"There. Now you can make all the scene you want and no one will hear."

"I don't want to make a scene," she whispered, her head buried in his chest.

"I do," André said, and reaching under her chin he tilted her head back and kissed her.

It wasn't a gentle kiss, but an all-consuming one. His lips slanted over hers, tasting, demanding a response and receiving one.

When he lifted his head, his eyes were dark and his breathing harsh.

"Did you mean what you said?" he asked.

"Huh?"

Rebekkah blinked, her gaze on his lips. An errant sniffle escaped, and she shuddered, trying to decide what he was talking about.

Instead of answering her he lowered his head and kissed her until her toes curled. "Say it again."

Blinking at him in utter amazement, she stared. Say what again?

Only then did she realize what she'd admitted out on the street. "I shouted that out there, didn't I?'' she asked, feeling warmth spread through her face.

"More like screamed it. I'm waiting to hear it again," he warned, his gaze focusing on her lips. "I wanted to hear it the other night but I didn't force you to say it. You needed time. But after what happened just now I'm not willing to wait any longer. That could have been you hit by the bullet as easily as it could have been me."

He started to lower his lips to hers, and she slipped a hand between them to stop him. One more kiss like that and she'd forget what she was supposed to say—again.

Looking into his eyes, she allowed all the love she felt to swell in her. "I love you, André, with all of my heart, my soul and my spirit. I love you."

Then she leaned forward. She placed her lips on his and returned the kiss he'd given her earlier.

When he finally broke it off she realized they were moving through the city streets in the car. Then she realized they were pulling into the hospital. She had no idea when the police officer had gotten into the front of the car or how he'd known where to take them.

She had no idea how far they'd traveled, either.

"Oh, dear," Rebekkah murmured and started worrying her lip. "Your dad." She was embarrassed that she'd allowed her emotions to rule her so she'd forgotten about Drydan.

André laughed, a full, deep, rich laugh. "My dad is fine. I admit I'm still shaken over what happened to him and nearly to me. But I wouldn't have let him get in the ambulance alone if I'd feared for his life."

"I didn't mean to take you away from him."

André smiled tenderly at her. "Honey, that reaction you gave me out on the street was the sweetest reaction I could ever have hoped for from the woman I love. Dad understood completely. Don't worry. Now, let's go in and see him."

Together they hurried into the hospital and found where Drydan was being treated. They went into the room and watched as his cheek was stitched up. The sheriff came in a short time later, and when the doctors were done with Drydan he told them all he knew about what had happened.

"Your stepson, Michael, knew what was going on. Evidently someone sent a memo to your mom about the cover-up. He heard her talking to a man here in Alaska named Ed. Ed wanted to get a copy of the memo so the case could be reopened. He remembered the memo he had sent to her and asked her to send it back so they could reopen this case. Evidently he felt that by hiding the evidence, which might have helped the other side, he might have been at fault for the possible cases of illness and death. At the time he evidently didn't believe Kittering was at fault, but later, something changed his mind. I have no idea what, and have a feeling this case is going to take a lot of time," the sheriff admitted.

Drydan shifted, dropping his legs over the side of the table. Standing he said, "My wife sent information to André so it'd come out. She thought it'd help heal the breach between us."

André sighed.

Rebekkah reached down and took the hand that wasn't around her waist and squeezed it, looking in sympathy at André.

"Evidently Michael didn't know that. He was worried if the information came out his mom would be hurt. He wasn't going to let that happen. He's confessed to several things, including the airplane incident, though he claims he didn't want it to crash. It looks like it'll take awhile to clear all of this up."

Drydan nodded. Standing in front of the sheriff, he said, "If he hasn't taken a lawyer yet I'd like to take on the job." He hesitated. "If that's okay with you, son." Drydan looked to André in question.

"He's related, so it might be hard." André faltered. "It might be best if you get someone to assist us with the case."

Drydan glanced sharply at his son.

"If you'll let me help, that is," André continued softly.

Rebekkah was certain she saw tears in Drydan's eyes as he cleared his throat and answered, "I'd be honored, son."

Rebekkah felt fresh tears in her eyes.

"Can it wait on me until I can go back with Rebekkah, though? She and I need to go visit some of her family."

André glanced at Rebekkah, looking into her eyes, searching her gaze for permission to bring up a subject she had guarded so carefully.

Rebekkah nodded. "It would mean a lot if you'd go with me, André. I'd like Mom to meet you."

André smiled. "It'd be nice to meet my future mother-in-law."

"You're engaged?" Drydan asked, stunned.

Rebekkah lifted an eyebrow. If he thought he was going to do that to her... "If we are, I don't know about it." She released André's hand and stepped back, crossing her arms in front of her chest.

André grinned. Dropping to one knee, he said softly, "I'd be honored if you'd consider marrying me and making me the happiest man in the world. I know this is an odd time to propose. So many things are up in the air, and it seems everything has fallen apart around us. But I believe God is in this. Everything is going to work out. And I'd like you to be there with me, by my side as we patch it all back together.''

Rebekkah smiled, joy building and spilling out in fresh tears. "I accept, André. If you can take me and all of my own life problems, together we can make it work.''

"With God.''

She nodded. "With God.''

André stood pulled her into his arms and kissed her.

Rebekkah thought that by admitting her love and accepting André's proposal, she had never been freer in her life.

Epilogue

The wedding was a quiet one. On one side Drydan seated André's mother. Behind them were guests. On the other side sat Rebekkah's mother and a newfound friend she'd discovered in church after she'd given her life to God. Behind them the pews were also filled with more guests.

Sarah, in her peach gown, was Rebekkah's matron of honor. Justin, in his black tux and blue cummerbund, was the best man. Mickie was the flower girl and was very proud of the fact as she went down the aisle tossing peach and white petals all over—the guests as well as the carpet.

Kittering had gotten out of the suit by agreeing to set up a fund for any family who had worked for Kittering or lived in the affected area in the years the suit called into question.

Michael would be out on probation in six months. André had refused to press charges, as had Rebekkah. So the charges against him were minor.

He was getting help inside and seemed to be doing much better.

It was Drydan's wife, however, who was doing the best. She'd had a breakdown after everything that happened. She was recovering and seemed so much better now that everything was out in the open.

She had started making quilts with her maid for the new babies born at their local church. It seemed to help her get back into the swing of life.

Rebekkah felt she had totally healed in the six months since everything had happened. She felt alive and new, fresh and ready to start a new life with the man who stood at the end of the aisle awaiting her.

Drydan finished seating his wife and came to her. Offering his arm, he smiled, and then slowly, together, they walked down the aisle.

As she walked she realized André was right. Everything had turned out well. With God in charge, anything was possible.

Drydan handed Rebekkah to André.

Rebekkah only had eyes for him as they said their vows.

And then those words she had thought never to hear in her lifetime, never to hear with this man. The pastor concluded the ceremony by saying, "I now pronounce you husband and wife."

She smiled.

"You may now kiss the bride."

And André did.

*   *   *   *   *

Dear Reader,

I just love André. You met him in *The Best Christmas Ever* (12/98) when he jilted Sarah. But I knew there was more to him than met the eye. I just wasn't sure what.

In the middle of the night, I finally knew what it was. André was so angry with his father that he went out on his own. He was willing to do anything to make his father admit what had happened was wrong. André needed a woman to help him to realize that holding back forgiveness can tear up a person's life. Rebekkah is that good, strong woman for André. But as you will see, she has her own set of problems.

The challenges I introduce aren't new to any of us. Hurt and pain, family strife—I don't know a family that hasn't gone through something. The key is forgiveness and moving on. When we learn to move on and let go, then God can bless our life—just like He blessed Rebekkah and André by bringing them together in marriage at the end.

Take a look in your heart today and find out what forgiveness you are holding back and let it go. And then stand back and watch what God will do.

As always, I love to hear from readers. P.O. Box 207, Slaughter, Louisiana 70777.

Blessings,

Cheryl Wolverton